TACKLED IN ⌐TACKS

A LOVE LETTERS PREQUEL

S.J. TILLY

LOVE
LETTERS

This book is dedicated to the BSU Library.
Only in my daydreams did something this exciting ever happen.

ONE
HANNAH – TUESDAY

"OPE, SORRY." I apologize unnecessarily as I jump to the side, narrowly missing the backpack sliding off some guy's arm.

He doesn't glance my way, blissfully unaware of our near collision, but the girl walking behind him rolls her eyes at his obliviousness.

Note to self: pay attention when walking.

With a clear sidewalk ahead of me, I glance down at the slip of paper in my hand.

It's the second day of classes, and I'm still learning my way around.

Yesterday went pretty okay. But my Monday-Wednesday-Friday schedule is different from the classes I have today and Thursday, so this is my first time walking this route during school hours. I've practiced a few times since I moved into my dorm room last week, but the campus seems different with so many people.

The energy is a lot to get used to.

I hook the thumb of my free hand under my backpack strap

as I make my way down the short set of stairs between two brick buildings.

In the midwestern September heat, there's a fine line between rushing and sweating, so I make myself walk at a normal speed. There's really no need for me to hurry. I'm not late, but I like taking my time picking a seat.

Voices fill the air as I enter the main quad.

It's a little intimidating, the quintessential image of college life before me, but I push aside my insecurities and try to soak in the moment.

I'm a student at HOP University.

Yesterday, my classes were at the other end of the campus, so I didn't really get this *first-day feeling*. And now that I'm here, it's a little overwhelming.

I worked my ass off in high school to finish with a few college credits to my name. And then I spent the last two years taking my generals at the community college in my hometown. But now... Well, now I'm a student here. And if I keep working my ass off, I can graduate with my accounting degree in three semesters. Which will set me up for a job that pays better than my mom's floral shop, and we can finally start to spoil ourselves.

And then I'll be able to pay off the student loans that have started to pile up around me.

A burst of laughter snaps me out of my thoughts, and I look up to see what can only be described as the *it crowd*.

I bat down another round of insecurities that try to bubble up inside me.

This is university life. People are less petty.

I can't help but think *I hope* as I let my eyes move over the group of students standing in a loose circle.

The guys are all wearing blue and black HOP U jerseys, and the girls are all in matching skirts and formfitting tops, with shoes that don't look comfortable for walking in.

I'm wearing jeans, a white T-shirt, and tennis shoes — because I don't want to start my week with blisters.

I felt pretty good about myself this morning, but the longer I look at this group of what must be sorority girls, the more that confidence slips away.

I'm a... bigger girl. Even when I tried to be a fanatic about counting calories. Even when I secretly bought those diet pills from the drugstore and hid them from my mom. Even when I made sure not to eat after nine p.m., I was still big.

Big boned.

Sturdy.

Built.

All the things people say instead of calling you chubby.

I bite my lip and pick up my pace again.

Those girls might be nice. Could be super kind. But being this close to them, when they look like *that* and I feel like *this*, is triggering all sorts of crappy internal chatter. And I don't need that. What I need is the credits I'll get for attending my macro-economics class.

"Mad Dog!" a male shouts, followed by a bad attempt at barking.

It's immature.

I don't want to smile.

I don't want to look over to see who *Mad Dog* is.

But my eyeballs don't care what I want.

A tall guy bounds forward, gripping the shoulders of an even taller guy, and jumps up like he's going to leap onto the guy's back.

My face scrunches up, waiting for the consequences. Because if someone did that to me, I'd fall flat on my face.

But that doesn't happen to *Mad Dog*. No, the giant, broad-shouldered guy doesn't budge. Not a single step forward.

My face goes from scrunched to impressed.

3

The guy, presumably Mad Dog, dislodges his friend, shaking his head.

But I miss whatever is said between them because I'm focused on how huge the guy is. Like, he's honestly the biggest man I've ever seen in person. I'm average height, but he... he has to be six and a half feet tall.

He's gotta be a student here. A football player, if I'm guessing the right sport for the jersey. But, seriously, how does a person get that big?

Realizing I'm gawking at his barrel chest, I blink and lift my eyes.

I can't have him, or anyone in the group, catch me staring.

He has dark stubble on his wide, square jaw that matches the color of his buzzed short hair.

If I had to describe my fantasy football player — and I mean fantasy like *fantasy*, not some made-up betting game — this guy would be it.

A real-life tall, dark, and handsome.

Even his eyes are a dark brown. And they're staring right at me.

My heart jolts behind my ribs.

One of those eyes closes, and he winks at me.

Heat flares up my neck, and I jerk my eyes away from his.

Cool, got caught eyeing the popular guy. Exactly what I was going for.

I force my shaky legs to pick up the pace as I redouble my efforts to get to class.

I'm not interested in any drama.

And a man called *Mad Dog* is bound to be drama.

TWO
MADDOX

I JAB my elbow back and shove Waller off me.

He shoves me back. "Senior year, bitch!"

I roll my eyes as I shake my head. You'd think our morning weightlifting session would have killed his energy, but nothing calms this fucker down.

The girls' laughter urges him on, so he keeps bouncing around, being a fool.

I'm not sure how this group of sorority chicks found us the second we got on campus, but I shouldn't be surprised. This particular group seems to be everywhere we go.

It's not like I have a problem with them. They've partied at the Football House over the last couple of years, but even though I live there, I don't know them beyond first names.

A feminine hand reaches for my chest, but Waller steps between us, slinging his arm around the girl's shoulders, derailing her attempt to touch me.

I don't like to be pawed at.

I'm no saint. No virgin. Haven't been since my senior year of high school.

And no shame to the guys who still like to cut loose every weekend, but I've had my fill of blurry nights.

I need to stay focused these last two semesters. I got too close to academic probation last year, and I can't get that close again. If I get pulled from the field my senior year, I'll be fucked.

Movement beyond our little crowd catches my attention, and I lift my eyes.

Across the way is a pretty girl with long honey-brown hair and plump bow-shaped lips.

Interest stirs in my ribcage.

I don't recognize her, but she doesn't look like a freshman.

And as I'm taking her in, I realize she's doing the same to me.

Her gaze is locked on my chest.

I'm a big dude. I stand out. I'm used to being looked at. But this? Her notice somehow feels deeper than surface level.

And if I straighten my back and tense my chest muscles, it's just a coincidence.

She's not a part of the current high-pitch crowd. And the plain shirt she's wearing shouldn't be sexy, but the way it stretches tight over her big tits fills me with the urge to cut the distance between us and press my face into the bright white fabric.

I drag my eyes up, noting her soft, round cheeks and the freckles across the bridge of her nose. A breath passes before her eyes lift and land on mine.

Her eyes widen, and I can feel her embarrassment over getting caught looking.

I can't help my humor, or my relief, at being the one who looked up first, so I do the only thing that feels appropriate.

I wink.

Pink hits her cheeks as she drops her gaze and hurries down the path.

My eyes follow her. And I can't help but notice how edible her ass looks in those jeans. The animal inside me begs me to chase her down. Except this tackle would be full of desire, not aggression.

But I don't follow her.

I can't.

I need to focus.

So, as the intriguing stranger rushes through the entrance of the econ building, I turn away.

I have my own class to get to.

THREE
HANNAH

"BEFORE THURSDAY, you need to read through the case study that starts on page twenty-seven." The ethics professor raises his voice as students close their books. "There will be a quiz, so don't blow this off."

His warning is met with a collective groan, but the professor just chuckles and tells us to have a good day.

I take my time sliding my things into my backpack.

Since I got to this class early — avoiding the quad at all costs after getting caught staring this morning — I overthought every aspect of my seat choice and ended up in the middle of the third row. Figured it was nice to leave the ends open for latecomers and the first rows open for the super students who like to be close enough to reach out and touch the teacher.

Once my row clears out, I stand and do the awkward sideways shuffle out of the narrow space.

I really hate the lecture halls that are set up like this. As if it's not bad enough that the seats themselves are made for skinny people from the 1940s, they also have to make the experience of getting *to* the seat its own sort of torture.

My sneaker catches on one of the chair legs. But the gods finally smile down on me, and I only tweak my ankle rather than falling onto the floor.

A win is a win.

Pressing my lips together, I take a deep breath through my nose.

This was my last class of the day, and I have forty minutes until my shift at the library, so I can take my time. No need to walk fast on my slightly throbbing ankle. No need to stress.

I melt into the sea of students leaving the building and squint when the afternoon sun lands on my face.

I take another slow inhale.

This is my new normal.

This campus. This schedule.

And I'm going to enjoy it.

I make it another dozen steps before the scent of cooking food wafts through the air.

Duh. How did I forget I have just enough time in my schedule to scarf down a late lunch before work?

I lift my gaze over the shoulders of the group ahead of me, trying to remember how I get to the cafeteria from here.

Left. Right. It all looks the same.

Seriously, why do the people who design college campuses have to make all the buildings identical?

Buildings...

I want to slap my hand to my forehead.

I went out the wrong exit.

I groan in annoyance as I spin around to go back the way I came.

But my groan turns into a croak when I crash into a body.

FOUR
MADDOX

AS I STEP out of my last class, I spot a white T-shirt I recognize.

My luck today keeps getting better.

I should turn right to head to the cafeteria, but before I can tell myself it's a bad idea, I head straight, following her.

My inner voice tells me I can't just approach a random girl because I think I saw her checking me out. But I shrug at myself. Because sure I can.

The swarm of students starts to fill in around my target, and not wanting to lose her, I start to jog.

I've just about reached her, my hand stretched out to tap her shoulder, when she twirls around and slams right into me.

FIVE
HANNAH

MY NOSE SMACKS into a solid chest, and I let out a pained sound, finally understanding the phrase *walked into a brick wall.*

Embarrassed but unable to stop it, my eyes immediately start to water.

"Sorry," I squeak as I start to teeter backward.

But before I can fall — into what I can only hope is an already dug grave — giant arms encircle me.

I don't fall.

I don't do anything.

I just stand there, stunned by the stinging pain in my nose, the throb in my ankle, and the fact that I'm being held upright by a stranger.

And, oh wow, he smells amazing. Like soap and cologne and exactly what I imagine someone in a magazine ad would smell like.

"Are you okay?" a deep voice rumbles from above my head.

Even as I nod, tears drip from my eyes, skyrocketing my humiliation.

11

"I'm fine." I try to project believability into my voice.

The hands pressing into my back slide up to my shoulders and hold me steady as he leans back a few inches.

"You sure?"

The man's voice is low and soothing, but as I'm lifting my gaze, I realize why I can *feel* his voice as well as hear it.

My hands are pressed against his chest.

His huge, wide, rock-hard chest.

The rough stitching under my palms makes me focus on what I'm looking at.

A jersey.

A HOP U football jersey.

Oh, please, no.

Holding my breath, I raise my eyes the rest of the way until they meet with the same dark irises that caught me staring just a few hours ago.

His mouth opens, a half smile pulling his lips to the side. But a moment later, his lips form a worried frown, and he's back to pulling me closer.

"Oh shit!" He slides one of his hands up from my shoulder to cup my cheek. "Aw, Babe, you're bleeding."

Babe?

My fingers curl against his chest.

So many things are happening right now. But none of them include me using words.

Am I dreaming? Did I fall asleep in that last lecture? Am I currently snoring alone in a lecture hall?

Up close, the man, Mad Dog, is even bigger than I first thought. Tall and broad and thick. I don't know much about football, but he's gotta be one of the biggest guys on the team. The ones who crash together like monster trucks.

I bet I could shove him as hard as I could, and he wouldn't fall over.

Not that I would do that.

I would never just shove a person.

A finger hooks underneath my jaw, and with a little pressure, he guides me to turn my face.

Too late, I remember my eyes are watering because of the impact, so I look like I'm crying.

I blink rapidly, trying to will them away, but instead, it causes a few more tears to break free.

His face lowers toward mine, and I have a split second to wonder if he's going to kiss me...

Then I remember this is real life, not a movie.

And did he say I was bleeding?

I yank my hands away from his body, which I should have done several seconds ago, and reach up toward my face.

"Wait." Before my fingers touch anything, he drops his hold on my chin and grabs both my wrists in his one big hand to stop me. "Your nose is bleeding. Fuck."

My eyes widen. "My nose?"

I've never had a bloody nose.

He nods. "I'm so sorry. Hold on."

"It was my..."

I was planning to say *fault*. Because it *was* my fault, not his. We both know it. But I can't finish my sentence because he's let go of me and is now reaching up under the hem of his jersey.

Is he going to take his shirt off?

There's a tearing sound, and then his hands reappear with a strip of gray cotton.

Did he...?

His eyes meet mine again. "I'm sorry," he says again. His frown deepens as he lifts his hand back to my cheek, only this time to wipe away a tear.

"Did you just rip off a piece of your shirt?" I'm practically whispering, and I don't know why.

He nods like it's perfectly normal to be able to rip a shirt to shreds when I know damn well I'd need some scissors to do what he just did.

"There's just a little..." He leans closer, stopping with his face inches from mine.

"I'm okay. I swear." I blink a few more times and reach up to brush away the lingering tears before he can. "I'm not crying."

The side of his mouth pulls up as he lifts the strip of shirt and dabs at the blood under my nose.

"I'm not." I catch another teardrop. "It just stings, is all."

His partial smile drops. "I'm really fucking sorry."

I huff, then wince. "It's not your fault. I shouldn't have stopped like that. I just... got turned around."

"Yeah, well, if I hadn't been right behind you like I was, we wouldn't have collided."

I shake my head the smallest bit. He's being nice, but he's wrong.

"Hold still." He grips my chin again, and I still. Even hold my breath.

He swipes below my nose once more. "I think it stopped. It was just a little bit."

The thumb against my cheek softly slides back and forth.

"Thanks." My lungs burn as I exhale.

He's so close.

"Where are you going?" His eyes hold mine.

Where am I...

I have to swallow before I can answer. "Work."

Technically, I spun around because I was going to go to the cafeteria, but now, I want to hide in a dark corner until my shift starts.

"Do you work in a restaurant?"

I slowly shake my head. "No, why?"

He grimaces. "I didn't mean for that to come off stalker-y or anything. Just that—" He gently brushes his thumb over my cheek once more before lowering his hands. "You should probably put some ice on your nose to make sure it doesn't swell. And if you worked in a restaurant..." He shrugs.

"Oh, uh, I work at the library." I stumble over my words.

It's so hard to think with him right *there* and smelling so good.

He stands up to his full height again, imposing but no longer crowding into my space, and glances over his shoulder. "I bet you could get some ice at the caf. They'd probably have a bag or something you could put it in."

I shake my head before he even finishes the thought. I don't think my heart could handle walking into the main cafeteria with this man. There would be too much speculation, from too many people, wondering what the big-deal jock is doing with the nobody nerd. And I don't want to deal with that if I don't have to. Especially since I'd be dealing with it while holding a bag of ice on my face.

He accepts my denial, probably thinking I don't have time. "If there's a vending machine at the library, get two cans of pop and press them here for a bit." He holds his pointer fingers vertically along the sides of his nose to demonstrate. "It'll help. Promise."

"If you promise." I blush the instant I say it. I'm not trying to flirt, but that sounded pretty flirty.

I shift my weight off my bad ankle and focus on breathing evenly.

He smirks. "I have some experience with these things."

"Crashing into girls?" I ask before I can stop myself.

His smirk turns into a smile. Like a *full* smile. And it's wild how good looking he is.

"I meant injured noses." He grips the front of his jersey and shakes it a little. "Defensive tackle."

My brows lift as I admit, "I don't know what that means."

He barks out a laugh, and the sound is rich and... happy.

But when he opens his mouth to say more, he's interrupted.

"Lovelace, you gettin' food with us?"

The big man, previously known to me only as Mad Dog, turns toward the voice.

When his attention is off me, I take a quick step back.

I need to get out of here before I do something worse than bleed on him.

Like drool on him.

With his back turned, I call out a quick "bye," then spin around and hurry down the path toward the library, cafeteria fully out of the question.

"Wait!" he shouts after me.

Not wanting to be rude but not wanting to stop, I lift a hand and wave over my shoulder. "Sorry!"

I'm not sure if I'm apologizing for crashing into him or for running away from him, but I figure he can take his pick.

SIX
MADDOX

FOR THE SECOND TIME TODAY, a pretty girl runs away from me.

The same girl.

A girl who didn't make any attempts to come on to me.

Maybe she's not interested.

If you promise.

The niggling feeling of rejection disappears when I think about the way she pressed her lips together after saying that to me.

And when I think about the way her fingertips pressed into my chest as I held her to me.

She's attracted to me. Has to be.

My teammate slaps his hand against my back. "You really know how to make the girls flee, don't ya?"

I shake my head, not answering, since he doesn't know how true that is.

SEVEN
HANNAH

I SMOOTH my dollar bill out on the edge of the vending machine.

"Pretty please, eat my money, you big block of parts," I grumble as I feed the bill into the slot for the third time.

The components whirl, and finally, my money disappears.

Double-checking, I press the correct buttons and wait for a can of Dr Pepper to drop out the chute. Then I repeat the process for a second can, and last, I select a granola bar. The bar will probably be a hassle to consume, but if I'm going to try to eat in secret, I need something that will fit in my pocket.

I'd roll my eyes at the irony of having a vending machine in the entryway to the library when you're not allowed to bring food inside, but it's coming in handy for me today, so I won't judge the lack of reasoning.

Slipping the bar into my jeans pocket, I tuck the two cans of pop into the crook of my arm and push the second set of heavy glass doors open.

As you'd expect, it's quiet.

The rattling HVAC system acts as a sort of white noise, making the large outdated space feel safe and comfortable.

The carpet is that thin industrial stuff that's barely softer than concrete, but it keeps my steps silent as I make my way behind the front desk and down the little hallway leading to the staff break room.

Inside the break room, lockers line one wall for our back-packs. A handful of tables and chairs that rarely get used litter the space, and a counter sits in the back corner with a sink, fridge, and microwave for anyone here long enough to require a lunch break.

My shifts are only four hours long, so I don't think I'll ever have an actual lunch in here. But...

I set the cans on a table and wedge my bag into my locker.

Looking at the cans, I blow out a breath.

This feels stupid.

Ridiculous.

But ending up with a pair of black eyes from walking into a man-wall would be worse than someone witnessing me holding cans to my face.

Four minutes later, I second-guess my choice when Sissy, a tiny woman with more energy than a caffeinated squirrel, appears in the doorway.

"Umm, what are you doing?" She half laughs.

I sigh and give the cans a quarter turn, trying to pull the last bit of coldness out of them. "I crunched my nose on, uh, some-thing, and supposedly, this will help stop it from swelling."

My face feels pretty much fine now. I don't know if it was the cans or just time, but either way, I'm confident I won't be left with any bruises.

Sissy hums. "That *something* have anything to do with a big, hot football player?"

I lower the cans to the table I'm sitting at and groan. "Please tell me you didn't witness it."

"No idea what you're talking about." She hooks a thumb over her shoulder. "But there's a ginormous football player who just walked in, asking me if the pretty girl in the white shirt" — she gestures to me — "with the long hair and freckles is feeling okay."

My brows raise, and I swear I can feel my eyes double in size. "He did not call me pretty."

Sissy nods. "He did. But I don't talk to strange men, so I pretended I didn't hear him and walked away."

A slightly manic laugh pops out of me.

Could it really be him coming here to check on me?

"You're serious?" I ask, just to make sure she's not messing with me.

She holds up three fingers, mimicking a scout's honor.

I have to snort.

Sissy works at the front desk, whereas I do book returns, but ever since I met her during the library orientation last week, I've liked her. She's basically the only friend I've made so far.

"So..." She twirls a finger in my direction. "I take it he has something to do with the Dr Pepper on your face?"

I grimace. "I *may have* run into him on my way here."

"And when you say run into...?"

"I mean, my clumsy ass literally ran straight into his body." I clap my hands together.

Sissy snickers. "How do you miss that guy? He's the size of a house. And how did you not break your face?"

I laugh. "One, I don't know. And two, I did break my face. Or at least my nose started to bleed."

She makes a face, and I get it.

On the way over here, I cut into another academic building

and checked myself in a bathroom mirror, relieved to see my face was blood free.

"Does that actually help?" She gestures to the cans in front of me.

I lift my shoulders as I scrunch my nose up, like I'm testing it. "Maybe?" Sighing, I push away from the table and stretch out my back as I stand. "I'm gonna stick these in the fridge, but if you want a can of Dr. Face, help yourself."

Sissy chuckles as she leaves, and I follow her out of the break room.

She wiggles her fingers in goodbye as she splits off to go behind the desk, and I go the other way to find my cart.

Sitting at the front desk and getting paid to do homework would've been ideal, but knowing Mad Dog Lovelace came in looking for me makes me a little glad to be on book-return duty.

It's nice of him to want to check on me, but I don't really know how to handle that sort of pitying attention.

With avoidance in mind, I select the cart with the most books and wheel it out of the room.

I'm not even halfway across the main floor — aiming for the elevators in the back — when I accept my mistake. The fullest cart is great for keeping me hidden in the stacks, but this particular cart is the one with a literal squeaky wheel. Meaning the cart is practically screaming my location as I cross the library.

Ignoring the racket, I keep my eyes focused on the floor just ahead of my cart, using my peripheral to watch for movement.

But I don't notice anyone walking toward me. No one gets up from any of the seating areas to approach.

The football player must have left.

Good.

But instead of feeling relieved, a tiny something pinches my heart.

EIGHT

MADDOX

DAMN. I didn't even need to be watching diligently. Pretty sure that squeaky-ass cart could've woken me from a dead sleep.

Instead of jumping out of my chair, I fight my chaser instincts and stay put.

Both times I've seen this girl, she's bolted. Run away like a frightened little bunny.

And I don't want to scare her. I want to... get to know her.

A few people glance her way, looking for the source of the noise, but she keeps her gaze on the ground.

I chose this spot because I can see the entirety of the long front desk. I assumed that's what she did here. It hadn't even occurred to me she could do something else. But this? This is perfect. Because now I can talk to her one-on-one. I don't have to stand at the desk with all her coworkers listening to our every word.

I look over to the desk and catch that same girl from before staring at me. The one who acted like I was invisible.

I almost smile, betting she went and found my girl to give her a heads-up.

But it doesn't matter if Bunny knows I'm here. I'm not trying to be sneaky. I'm also not going to give up.

The squeak stops, and I turn my attention back to my mystery girl.

From twenty feet away, I watch the side of her mouth pull down into a little frown. Then she steps around her cart and presses the button to call the elevator.

I sit forward.

The elevator doors slide open.

I set down the magazine I was pretending to read.

She pushes her noisy-ass cart forward.

I stand.

She turns around and presses the button for the floor she wants.

I take a step forward.

Her eyes lift. And meet mine.

The elevator doors slide shut.

NINE
HANNAH

OH GOD.

I press my hand against my chest, over my heart.

He's still here.

The floor counter ticks up slowly.

What should I do?

It takes me half a second before I roll my eyes at myself.

What I should do is put books away. Because it's my job. Because I need the money. And because I can't let myself get distracted by the first hot guy to give me attention.

And it's not like he's really *giving me attention.*

He saw me staring at him.

He was innocently walking between classes when I smashed into him.

And his coming here to make sure I didn't bleed to death in the last half hour doesn't count as *attention.*

The elevator cab starts to slow as it reaches the top floor.

He'll probably leave now that he's seen I'm fine.

24

TEN
MADDOX

MY FEET THUD as I hurry up the final flight of stairs to the fourth floor.

I might be an athlete, but I'm not exactly stealthy. So when I hear the ding of the elevator above me on the fourth floor, I slow my ascent.

It's not like I need to have eyes on her since I can hear her cart from here.

At the end of last year, when my grades started to slip, I spent a fair amount of time in the study rooms on the second floor, but I also came up here a time or two to find a book for an assignment.

It's a mostly unused floor, so it's quiet. But there is a pair of chairs in the far corner that I got to know fairly well.

They're boxy armchairs, and they aren't the most comfortable things, but I have fallen asleep in them once or twice. And most importantly, they're in the direction she's heading.

I take a sharp right — away from the squeak — and circle around the other end of the shelves. If I hurry, I can get to those chairs before she circles the last stack.

Staying on the balls of my feet, I move as quietly as I can down the end aisle.

I'm perpendicular to the stacks, but with the noisy wheel, I know when I'm nearly across from her. If I don't time it right, she'll see me through the aisle.

Lengthening my stride, I cross the next gap in two steps.

When she doesn't call out, and the cart doesn't stop moving, I let out my exhale.

But I don't slow down.

ELEVEN
HANNAH

NOTE TO SELF: don't listen to any more of Mom's ghost stories.

It's not that the library is scary. It's just that, well, it's a little scary.

With the high rows of shelves... the limited sightlines... the quiet... it feels like another realm sometimes.

I look over my shoulder.

The feeling of being watched crawls over my skin as my heart skips a beat, but it's just nerves after seeing *him* here.

Slowing, I peek at the books on the cart to verify the number on the spines.

The carts are stacked to match the floors. The books for the top floor on the top rack of the cart, and so on and so forth.

I change my grip on the cart and pull it to a stop at the third row from the end, then grab the two books that need to get put away here.

In the silence, I try to listen for any signs of someone approaching, but there's nothing.

Quit being a baby.

Putting all thoughts of ghosts and football players out of my mind, I focus on the shelves and slide the first book into its spot. When I reach up to put the second book away, my pocket crinkles, and I remember the granola bar.

I quickly shove the book into place, then pull the package out of my pants pocket.

"Well, crap." Through the wrapper, I can tell the crunchy bars inside have broken in half.

These really are the worst of all the granola bars. I don't know why I even got it.

Then my stomach grumbles.

Right. I got it because I missed lunch.

I eye the cart at the end of the aisle, then the granola bar.

My shift has barely started, but no one will know if I take a little break to eat. And maybe, as a side effect, the lingering adrenaline I've had since smashing my face against Mad Dog will finally go away.

Leaving the cart where it is, I exit out the other side of the aisle, turn toward the back corner with the chairs, and nearly have a heart attack.

TWELVE
MADDOX

SHE STEPS out from her row, turns in my direction, and throws something at my face.

I might not be a wide receiver, but my hand snaps up on reflex, and I snatch the granola bar out of the air.

Her hands are pressed against her chest like she's trying to keep her heart inside her body, and her eyes are wider than I would've thought possible.

"Sorry." Her voice is high pitched. "I didn't mean to..."

She trails off, and I have to chuckle. "You didn't mean to chuck this brick at my face." I open my palm and look down at the package. "I didn't think people actually ate these."

She drops her hands. "I wasn't really looking forward to it."

"Don't tell me this is your lunch?"

She lifts a shoulder.

I lean forward in the chair. "I was about to eat. If you'd like to share."

I want to get up and walk to her, but I'm kind of a giant compared to her, and sitting keeps me more on her level.

She presses her teeth into her pink lower lip. "Is that what you're doing here?"

"A little lunch. A little first aid follow-up." I raise an eyebrow. "So... lunch?"

She shakes her head. "I don't think I should."

Not I don't want to.

"You're hungry, though, yeah?" I give the green wrapper a little shake.

"Yeah, but I can just have that." She points to the crumbly-as-shit granola bar she chucked at my head.

"This is rabbit food." I smirk at my own inside joke. "You need more than that."

"It's fine. I —"

Before she can argue more, I tighten my grip on the wrapper, crushing the hard bars inside into pieces.

"Hey!" She takes a step toward me.

Victory.

"One sec." I hold up a finger, rip open the top of the package, lift it to my lips, and tip my head back, dumping the contents into my mouth.

When I lower my head back to look at her, I find her another step closer with her mouth open in disbelief.

"That was mine," she accuses.

"You threw it at me. Makes it mine."

She purses her lips. "I don't think that's a real thing."

"Well, either way, you have to eat with me now."

She props her hands on her hips, and I have to force my eyes to stay on her face. "How am I supposed to eat with you when you just inhaled my food?"

"Inhaled?" I press a hand to my chest. "I'm insulted." She rolls her eyes at me, and it's way cuter than it should be. "And lucky for you, I eat a lot."

She gives me a look. "How is that lucky for me?"

"Because." I reach down next to my chair and drag my backpack over so it's in front of me. "I have an extra sandwich." I unzip the main compartment. "You like ham and cheese?"

THIRTEEN
HANNAH

WHAT. *Is. Happening?*

The big man proceeds to pull out three individually wrapped sandwiches that I recognize from the cafeteria.

"Yeah," I answer slowly. *Who doesn't like ham and cheese?*

He holds one out to me. "Here, I don't need all three."

"How'd you know I'd be on this floor?" I have to ask. "And how'd you beat me?"

He grins. "Lucky guess. And" — he uses a sandwich to gesture at himself — "athlete, remember?"

I eye the sandwich as my stomach grumbles again.

Sighing, I step forward. "Since you ate my —"

My words cut off when he bolts out of his seat.

"Are you still hurt?" The Athlete closes the few feet between us in a blink, the sandwiches thumping to the floor as he grips my shoulders.

A startled sound leaves me.

"Why are you limping?"

"What —" *Oh, right, that.* "I'm fine."

He makes a growling sound, then his hands drop down to my waist.

With brute strength, the man lifts me and turns us around.

"Sit," he commands even as he starts to set me down in the chair angled toward his.

I bend my legs, no choice but to do what he says, and sit down.

The second my butt hits the seat, he crouches before me.

He slides his hands down my hips, stopping on my knees. "Is this because of me?"

"No." I hold up my hands, palms out. "It isn't."

"Did someone hurt you?"

His tone is so serious I can't help but widen my eyes.

"What? No. Look, I tripped walking out of class and tweaked my ankle," I admit, watching his eyes drop to my feet. "It's embarrassing, but it's true."

He makes an unconvinced humming sound.

"When my cans of pop cool off again, I'll press them to my ankle."

His scowl finally softens. "You did it for your nose?"

I nod. "Some guy told me it would help."

"Some guy, huh?"

"Yeah. Tall, hard to miss. Wolfed down my granola bar in two chomps."

"Wolfed down?" he repeats.

I nod. "You kinda did."

He smirks, and I hope he can't hear my pulse pounding through my veins. "That make me the big bad wolf to your little bunny?"

"Little bunny?" I don't know if anyone has ever called me little before. Then again, compared to the man in front of me, I actually am.

"Need to call you something. And you're always running away from me, like a little bunny."

I bite my lip, loving that he's given me a nickname.

"So..." He drags out the word. "What's your name?"

It's a normal question, but for some reason, it makes me blush.

I force my hand out between us. "I'm Hannah."

His smile is slow and full of mischief. "Hi, Hannah."

Electricity zaps down my spine as he slides his hand against mine, saying my name.

"I'm Maddox."

FOURTEEN
MADDOX

"MADDOX." The way she says it makes it sound like she's tasting it. Like she's getting a feel for it. And she likes it.

Her palm is so soft and smooth against mine. And it fits perfectly.

"Nice to officially meet you." I force myself to let go of her knee and pick up one of the sandwiches off the carpet. "Can I offer you a floor sandwich?"

Hannah lets out a small exhale of laughter. "Yes, please."

I set the clear-wrapped food in her lap, then snag the other two and push up to standing.

I'm a little sore from squats this morning, so I have to shake my legs out as I move back to the chair.

After I drop into my seat, we start unwrapping our meals at the same time.

"We're not supposed to eat in here," Hannah says as she holds the ham and cheese a few inches from her lips.

I shove my sandwich into my mouth, taking a large bite. "It's alright. I know a girl who works here."

She shakes her head at my dumb joke, but then she takes a bite too.

We each take another before I ask, "So, Hannah, you new here?"

FIFTEEN

HANNAH

I NOD. "Just transferred. I'm a junior."

Maddox dips his chin. "Senior. What's your major?"

Calmness radiates off him, and I start to relax.

"Accounting. You?" I take another bite of my sandwich.

It's good, better than it should be. And I'm trying really hard not to feel weird about eating in front of a guy I don't really know.

"Business administration. Something passable and useful," he answers. "You want to be an accountant?"

"Yeah." I shrug.

He snorts. "Not convincing me, Hannah."

Since he answered me honestly, I decide to do the same. "Something hirable and pays well."

I didn't grow up poor. My mom owns a little flower shop, and it does well enough to cover the basics. But I want to be able to help her with the books. And I want to get a job I can support myself with, sooner rather than later. Because I love my mom, but I want to move out. I want to have new experiences.

Maddox balls up his wrapper and rips open the second sandwich.

Glancing down into his open backpack, I see a book I recognize. "You reading that for a class?"

He follows my line of sight. "Uh-huh. You've read it?"

I nod. "It's one of my favorite stories."

A look crosses his face that I don't know what to do with, and I decide it's time for me to leave.

Nothing good can come from getting to know Maddox. Either I'll learn he's a douchebag, and then I'll start to hate him, which would suck, or I'll learn his personality is just as enticing as his appearance, and then I'll be really fucked.

Because if it's the latter, I'll be forming a crush, while he'll accept my nose isn't broken and forgive himself.

And then I'll never see him again.

The numbers don't add up.

There's no good outcome here.

I rewrap what's left of my ham and cheese and stand.

"I should really get back to work." I'm being abrupt and rude, but Maddox doesn't point it out.

"I suppose you're on the clock." He looks at his watch. "I gotta head over to practice anyway."

Unlike me, saving my leftovers, he shoves the remainder of the second sandwich into his mouth.

He stands and slings his bag over his shoulder, then gestures down toward my feet. "You sure your ankle is okay? You shouldn't be working if it hurts."

I take a few stationary steps. "See? It's okay."

His mouth thins, but he just sighs instead of arguing. "Alright, Hannah Bunny."

At a loss for how to respond, I give him a nod, then take the few steps to the row where my cart is waiting.

"Take care of yourself," he tells me.

I pause. "Bye, Maddox."

It sounds like a farewell.

Ignoring the pit that forms in my stomach, I listen to his retreating steps and focus my thoughts back on what's important.

Because swooning over the hot football player isn't important.

SIXTEEN
MADDOX – WEDNESDAY

I FIND her on the second floor this time. Standing on a step stool, a book in each hand, reaching to put them away on the top shelf.

My protective instincts are something else around this girl. Because instead of staring at her ass — which is very stare-able in those tight jeans — I'm completely focused on her apparent lack of self-preservation.

Clenching my teeth so I don't reprimand her, I quickly cross the distance between us.

Hannah doesn't even hear me approach. Her attention is focused on the book she's trying to push into place with her right pointer finger while her left arm is stretched out in the other direction for counterbalance. She should've gotten down, moved the stool, and climbed up again. But no. Not this girl. She'll just *make it work*.

It's as if I can smell her stubbornness.

That thought almost makes me smile. My parents are always calling me stubborn. Maybe that's why I'm so drawn to Hannah. A part of me can tell she'd be a worthy partner — and opponent. She might be a little nervous around me now, but if we were together, she wouldn't let me get my way all the time.

And that appeals to me.

It appeals to me a lot.

She starts to teeter.

Her right hand releases the book and grips the shelf for balance. But the book wasn't pushed in far enough, and it starts to slip out.

I know what she'll do before she even does it, so I'm already jogging the final yards when she lets go of the shelf to catch the book.

Her left hand blindly slaps against the shelf, but she's still holding a book in that hand too.

"Dammit, woman," I grit out as I duck under her outstretched arm.

She tips right into me.

Those pretty brown eyes blink down at mine. "Maddox?"

I wrap my arm around her waist. "Didn't I tell you to take care of yourself? Like yesterday?"

"Sorry." Her apology is breathy, and before I know what I'm doing, I turn her into me, bringing us chest to chest.

Her arms automatically circle around the back of my neck, and I pull her the rest of the way off the stool.

Something thumps to the ground behind me, and then her arms tighten around my shoulders, her hands clutching my bunched muscles.

Fuck, she feels good in my arms.

I tighten my hold on her.

It's a full-body hug with her feet dangling off the ground. And I want her to wrap those legs around me.

I want to shove her back against the bookshelves.

I want to press my mouth to hers.

I want to see what she tastes like.

"Wh-what are you doing?"

Her breath puffs across my lips, and I swear it smells like oranges.

"Saving your life, apparently." My answer is gruff, making me sound angry.

But really, I'm just gritting my teeth, trying to will my cock to settle down. Because standing like this, with her soft, warm body flush against mine, is hard. The temptation. My dick. It's all hard.

"Um." Her tongue darts out to wet her lips. "Thank you?"

Knowing I can't keep holding her like this — because I'll end up doing something I'm sure she's not ready for — I loosen my arms, letting her slide down my front.

Bad idea.

Her tits drag down my chest, the pair of T-shirts between us doing nothing to hide the soft feeling of them against my firmer body.

I tilt my hips back, just a little, just enough so she doesn't get a belly full of dick.

Then I have to fight down a groan because now I'm thinking about giving her an actual belly full of my dick, thinking about stripping us both down right here and rutting her into the carpet.

Hannah's feet hit the floor, and I clear my throat. "How, um, is your nose okay?"

Her cheeks are so red, her eyes so focused on mine, I know she felt my hardness against her. And I know she's trying her best to keep her gaze on my face.

She gives her head a tiny shake. "Doesn't hurt at all."

Part of me wants her to glance down. To take a peek at the bulge in the front of my pants. But then I remember I'm not a fucking pervert, so I tuck my hands into my pockets and try to act like a decent human.

"Good. I'm glad." I rock back on my heels. "And your ankle?"

She glances down.

It's fast. So fast I'd have missed it if I blinked. But I didn't miss it. And I don't miss the way her cheeks turn even redder.

I have to stop myself from grinning.

"It's fine." Her voice comes out high pitched, and she swallows. "Totally better."

"Happy to hear that." I dip my chin. "If you can get through the whole day without falling off a stool, then you might be okay tomorrow too."

She huffs, and the tension pops between us.

Just like that.

From lust to comfort in a heartbeat.

The lust is still there. It's definitely there. But this feeling...

I step closer to her before I can think better of it.

I like this feeling I get when I'm around her.

"I'm not usually this clumsy," she tries to tell me, making the side of my mouth tip up. "I'm not."

"Sure." I raise my brows.

She rolls her eyes. "I'm not. Maybe it's you." She waves her hand in my direction, her eyes staying on mine. "You throw me off."

That makes me smile. "You didn't even know I was here."

"Yeah, well..." She trails off.

"Good point." I nod.

This time, I get a real laugh out of her.

"Oh, shut up." She smacks my chest with the back of her hand, then she yanks her hand back like I'm made of lava and widens her eyes. "Sorry! I don't know... I didn't mean to do that."

"It's alright." I grab her forearm and, using my grip, make her smack me again. "See?"

She bites her lip that way she does, but I see her smile.

Before she can run away, I ask her the question that's been clinging to me since yesterday. "Are you going to the game tomorrow night?"

"What ga—" She starts, then looks at my chest like she can see the jersey I was wearing yesterday. "The football game?"

I can tell she has no idea that we play tomorrow. And I kinda enjoy that.

"Yeah, the football game."

"I wasn't planning on it. No offense or anything," she adds quickly. "I just hadn't... I've never been to one before."

"Never?"

"I've seen some on TV."

I grin. "Well, would you like to see one in person? Tomorrow?"

"Um, sure? I mean . . ." She glances away. "If the tickets aren't super expensive."

Something twists in my chest.

I'm not responsible for this girl. And she's not asking me for anything. But I hate that the cost of the ticket would be her deciding factor.

"I have an extra one," I explain. "All the players get a few."

She stares up at me. "And you want to give it to me?"

"Don't sound so confused, Bunny."

Her mouth opens, then closes as her shoulders drop. "It was all my fault yesterday. I realized I wanted to go to the cafeteria and that it was the other way, and — I dunno. I'm dumb. So I just turned around, not thinking about the fact that people were everywhere, and that's why I ran into you."

My forehead furrows. "It wasn't dumb. It was an accident."

"But still. I just — You don't have to feel bad. It wasn't your fault I got..." She waves her hand in front of her face. "I promise I'm okay and that you don't owe me anything."

There it is.

"Ah, I see."

She shrugs. "So you can give the ticket to someone else if you want. We're good."

This girl.

Every sentence out of her mouth makes me want to spend more time with her. I wish I could sit with her at the game rather than ask her to come alone, but knowing she's there will have to be enough.

"Here's the thing," I explain. "It kind of was my fault." I hold up a hand before she can argue. "Because I was *really* close behind you. And I was really close behind you because I was chasing after you."

She blinks. "You were chasing me?"

I tip my head side to side. "Chasing sounds bad, but yeah, basically."

She scoffs.

"I was." I lower my hands. "I spotted you walking ahead of me, and I wanted to... talk."

"Am I supposed to believe this?" Her tone is so incredulous it makes me want to laugh.

"It's the truth, Babe." Wanting to see her cheeks bloom red again, I say the rest of it. "When I caught you checking me out that morning, you snagged my attention."

On cue, her face flushes. "I was not."

"It's okay." Like a jackass, I lift and flex both my arms, puffing out my chest. "I get it."

That makes her snort. "You're such a jock."

"And you like it." I grin. "Now tell me you'll come to my game."

Hannah heaves out a breath. "What time is it?"

"What time are you done with work?" I ask, assuming she's working tomorrow too.

She narrows her eyes at me. "Six."

"Good. Game starts at seven. Plenty of time to hobble over to the field."

She picks up her feet, walking in place like she did for me yesterday. "I don't need to hobble."

"Even better."

"Okay, fine. I'll come to your game." She holds out her hand.

I love that she calls it *my* game.

I take her hand in mine and shake on it.

She snickers and keeps her hand up when I let it go. "I meant for you to give me the ticket."

I look at her palm, and a burst of laughter breaks out of my chest.

It's so loud she steps into my space and pokes my stomach. "Shh!"

I lean into her fingertip. "Not sure why, but I kinda like it when you scold me."

She pulls back her finger and pokes me again.

I chuckle, quieter this time. "I don't have the tickets on me, but you can pick them up at the will call window outside the gates."

Her mouth forms an O of understanding. "Gotcha."

"I just need to give them your last name, and then you'll need to show them your student ID."

She purses her lips for a moment before she replies. "Utley."

"Utley," I repeat.

"And it's Hannah. In case you forgot."

Slowly, I shake my head. "I didn't forget, Hannah Utley." I reach up and slide my fingers over a strand of her long, soft hair. "My last name is Lovelace." I know she remembers my first name because she's already said it to me.

I take a step back, the piece of hair falling from my grip and back onto her shoulder.

I don't want to leave, but I need to get to practice. "Will call. Tomorrow."

Then I see the books she dropped, and I pick them up and hand them to her.

"Thank you. And thank you for the ticket."

I take another step back. "You'll cheer for me." I don't ask it.

"Of course." She gives me a serious nod. "Or at least, I'll cheer when everyone else does because I have no idea what the rules are." A smirk plays at the side of her mouth, and I want to kiss it.

"Bye, Utley."

Her fingers wiggle at her side. "Bye, Lovelace."

SEVENTEEN
HANNAH - THURSDAY

HOLY. Shit.

I rub my palms against my thighs.

I knew college football was a thing. Like a big thing. But I still wasn't prepared.

The crowd around is *screaming*. The game hasn't even started, yet they've been screaming since the teams ran into the stadium in a blur of band music and cheerleaders.

What in the hell did I get myself into?

A guy next to me jumps into the air, startling me, and I press my hands against my stomach.

Why am I so nervous?

The starting players run out onto the field, and my stomach does another somersault.

I don't know why I'm pretending to myself. I'm nervous because I'm here to watch Maddox play.

Maddox, the sandwich-sharing *defensive tackle* who has lifted me — twice — like I weigh nothing. The man who seems to be built from stone but who I don't want to watch get hurt.

I force myself to take a slow breath through my nose.

I know the most basic of basics when it comes to football. I know a touchdown is six points. And I'm fairly certain it's called a field goal when they kick it through the post things. But I also know it's dangerous. And violent. And... I press my hands harder against my stomach.

Breathe.

A girl a few rows ahead of me, dressed in blue and black like the rest of the crowd, holds a sign high above her head. The back is blank, but after she bounces a few times, she turns around so the sign faces the rest of the student section.

HOP ON

Mad Dog

#99

It takes focus not to scowl at her sign.

Does she have a history with Maddox? Or is she just trying to do a play on words?

I drag my eyes away from the sign and look at the girl again.

She looks... familiar.

Was she a part of the crowd Maddox was standing with that first time I saw him?

Dozens of people start chanting *Mad Dog*, and I suddenly feel even more out of place than I did before.

I might not admit it out loud, but that girl's sign fills me with jealousy.

I have no right to feel that way. He's not mine. And even if he were, there's nothing wrong with classmates, or fans, holding up signs.

I'm happy Maddox has so many people cheering him on.

Inhaling through my nose again, I try to calm my nerves.

The student section, where I'm seated — in name only, since everyone is standing — is filled with tangible energy. While I soak it in, I focus on the important information from the sign. Maddox is number ninety-nine.

The home bench is across the field from where I am, and with helmets and all the padding the players wear, I couldn't tell which one was Maddox.

I mean, I assume he's the biggest guy on the team, but that's just an assumption. And now I can focus on looking for his number.

A whistle blows, and the HOP U team moves as one.

The guy in the center kicks the football, and the team sprints down the field.

Students are jumping around, blocking my view, making it hard for me to see the players, let alone read their jerseys.

The other team catches it, and then they're all running toward each other.

I feel sick.

One of our players tackles the guy with the ball, and a whistle is blown.

Just breathe, Hannah.

I spent some of my shift today looking up football terms and rules, but I'm still so lost.

Someone in the ridiculous HOP U mascot costume runs down the sideline in front of us, a giant school flag in his hands. Why our mascot is a panda, I'm sure I'll never know.

The students hoot and holler at the woodland creature, but I keep my attention on the field.

I squint, trying to read the numbers as the team huddles together. I'm about to turn my attention to the guys standing on the side of the field, because maybe Maddox isn't playing right now, but then the huddle breaks. And I see it.

Him.

Even at a distance, he's intimidating.

The teams line up facing each other. Maddox is right in the middle of everything, staring into a sea of opposing players decked out in green.

My adrenaline kicks into overdrive.

I don't like this.

A guy in green hikes the ball.

Both lines move.

Maddox crashes into an opposing player nearly as big as he is.

I really don't like this.

They shove at each other.

Maddox breaks free.

The quarterback throws the ball.

Maddox changes direction.

The ball is caught.

Another whistle blows.

My shoulders sag, and I pull the front of my bright white tank top away from my body, trying to get some air.

I don't know how people watch their loved ones play this game.

Not that Maddox is my loved one.

I barely know him.

Once again, the teams line up.

How long are these games?

My eyes lock on to Maddox's extra-large frame.

The crowd is still standing. People are still screaming.

They can't keep this up the entire game, right?

Except they do.

EIGHTEEN
MADDOX

SHE'S HERE.

I can't find her in the crowd. That's practically impossible. But Hannah is here. I can practically feel her eyes on me.

"Let's fucking go!" Waller shoves me as we come out of the huddle and line up.

Let's fucking go.

We're up by three.

It's the fourth quarter.

It's fourth down.

There's less than a minute left on the clock, and these dumb assholes are giving up the field goal that would tie it to go for the touchdown.

Being cocky only works if you're the best.

I bend my knees and lean forward, touching my hand to the field.

Scouts are always watching.

But tonight, my Bunny is watching too.

And this is her first football game.

I want her to remember it.
I want her to remember me.
Because these fools aren't the best.
I am.
The other team hikes the ball.

NINETEEN
HANNAH

MY THROAT IS raw from cheering. My feet are sore from standing on the metal bleachers. And my hands are still sweating.

We're currently ahead. The time is almost out. And I've listened to enough people around me to know that the other team is trying to win the game.

And they're trying to win it right now.

The player across from Maddox snaps the ball back, and Maddox takes off.

He's fast.

Faster than a guy his size should be.

Just as he's about to collide with the other team's player, he shifts. Instead of hitting him head-on, their shoulders clip, and Maddox spins around him.

Everyone around me screams.

Shouts of "*Get him*" and "*Sack him*" and "*Mad Dog*" ring through my ears.

But I don't make a sound because my voice is stuck in my throat.

There's no one between Maddox and the quarterback.

No one to stop him.

The opposing quarterback takes quick steps backward away from Maddox.

And I get it now.

I understand why they call my big, friendly guy Mad Dog. Because right now, he looks feral.

With a deafening roar from the crowd, Maddox plows into the quarterback.

Everyone around me is jumping.

Cheering.

Except Maddox doesn't go down with the quarterback.

"Oh fuck!" the guy next to me shouts.

It's like the stadium takes a breath, a beat of silence, as the quarterback falls and Maddox scoops the ball off the ground.

My hands fly to my mouth.

This feels big.

Maddox starts running.

This feels really big.

Ball in hand, Maddox starts running down an empty field.

The players in green are chasing him, but the ones in blue are shoving them over. Pushing them away. Keeping the path clear for Mad Dog Maddox.

I press my hands harder over my mouth.

Go, go, go!

The floor beneath me trembles with excitement.

My heart is beating out of control.

And then he's crossing the line.

Maddox is in the end zone.

The time's up.

He just scored a touchdown.

And we won.

Tears fill my eyes as the HOP U players surround Maddox.

My chest is so tight. I'm so... Fuck, I don't even know what this feeling is. It's like so much happiness is trapped inside my rib cage that it's squishing my lungs.

I'm so thrilled for him.

So proud of him.

So... in awe.

The girl behind me screeches and grabs my shoulders, giving them a shake. "Did you see that?"

I nod.

It's all I can do.

As the team jogs back toward the bench, Maddox looks this way, into the student section, at the hundreds of people. And it feels like he's looking right at me.

Behind my hands, I smile.

TWENTY
MADDOX

PUSHING away from the kitchen table, I stand and stretch out my back.

"Mad Dog," a guy I recognize shouts at me over the thumping music.

I tip my head back in acknowledgment, then pick my Gatorade up off the table.

Sometimes I love living in the Football House. Sometimes I enjoy the parties. But it's not what I want tonight.

What I want works in the library.

What I want is a girl who blushes while she teases me.

What I want is to have that girl in my arms again.

In my arms.

In my bed.

Marked as mine.

Adjusting myself, I shake out my leg, then try to make my way through the bodies crowding the main floor, but it's fucking elbows to assholes in here.

"Coming through!" I snap.

It's too loud for anyone to catch the true annoyance in my tone. But people still part for me, lifting hands for high fives.

I don't mind being a big person.

I need to be big to play the way I do.

But when you're my size — wearing triple XL clothing, standing nine inches taller than the average man — it's not exactly easy to *slip through* anywhere.

Elbows are bumped. Drinks are sloshed. But I finally make some progress.

I'm almost to the stairs when someone steps in front of me.

"Hey, Maddox." Essie stops right in my path.

"Hey," I reply and try to move around her.

"You heading upstairs?" She looks up at me, an expression on her face that says she wants to join me.

The second floor is bedrooms and strictly invite only.

Essie is your classic *it girl*. Always looks perfect. Always dresses as though a paparazzo might take her photo. She's attractive.

But her hair is the wrong shade of brown.

She doesn't have any freckles.

And I don't feel even the smallest urge to ask her questions about her life.

"I am," I answer, and her innocent smile starts to pull into a smirk. But then I speak again. "Good night."

She tries to cover her annoyance over the rejection, but I see the way her lips pinch together. "Night."

I'm not trying to be rude, but I'd rather be blunt than lead a girl on. She's been spending a lot of time hanging around the team. So it's best to put an end to any of her hopes now.

Spotting Waller a few feet away, I call out his name. He knows I don't drink during the season, but if I disappear without telling him I'm going to bed, he'll come searching for me later to make sure I'm okay.

He's a good friend.

He puts his thumbs in his armpits and flaps his arms like chicken wings.

He's also an idiot.

"Nate!" I shout louder, and he finally snaps his head in my direction.

I point up the stairs.

He pulls one of his thumbs out of his armpit and holds it up for me.

Then he makes a face like he smells something bad, and I shake my head and start up the stairs.

This is why I need my little library girl.

I need some class in my life.

TWENTY-ONE

HANNAH

REACHING UP, I flip off the little lamp I have clipped to the bedframe.

Darkness falls inside my dorm room, and I'm more thankful than ever that I have a single room. I couldn't deal with a roommate right now. Not feeling like this.

It's been hours since the game ended, and even though I'm exhausted, I'm thrumming. The energy of the crowd was just so much.

I place my palm over my heart as I settle onto my back.

My thoughts go to Maddox. They've been on him since, well, basically, since I first laid eyes on him. And definitely since he held me yesterday.

His body felt so solid against mine. He felt so sturdy. Like nothing could hurt me — nothing could even touch me — with him there.

I close my eyes. The darkness changes to images of him.

That strong jaw covered in stubble that would scratch the corners of my mouth if he ever kissed me.

The short hair covering his head that I want to run my fingers through.

Those big hands that I want to touch me. That I want *everywhere*.

The hand over my heart slides down... And under my palm, my nipple is already hard.

I think about the way Maddox looks into my eyes like he can see all of me.

My fingers squeeze around my breast.

I think about his arms wrapped around my waist.

My other hand slides across my belly toward the top of my sleep pants.

I think about the hardness pressing into my stomach when he lowered me.

My fingers move into my panties.

I think about what it might be like to be in bed with Maddox Lovelace.

TWENTY-TWO
MADDOX

AFTER DOUBLE-CHECKING that my door handle is locked, I flip off the lights and take the few strides across my tiny room to my bed.

The frame creaks as I drop onto the mattress.

My blankets are still flung back from this morning, but instead of pulling them over me, I kick them out of the way.

I've learned to sleep through anything, so I don't mind the music vibrating through the house.

But I'm not going to sleep.

Not yet.

I grip my hardening dick through my boxers.

And picture Hannah.

Picture what she must have looked like standing in the bleachers.

Imagine the way she'd have thrown her arms around my neck if I'd been able to find her after the game. Remember the way her perfect, soft body felt against mine.

Shoving my waistband down, I wrap my fingers around my length.

And I think about how well she'd take me.

I think about it in detail.

The sounds she'd make.

The way she'd dig those fingernails into my shoulders.

How she'd bounce with each thrust. How I wouldn't have to worry about hurting her. How I could be myself with her.

I close my eyes, and I think about Hannah Utley.

TWENTY-THREE
HANNAH – FRIDAY

"DO YOU WORK THIS WEEKEND?" Sissy startles me by popping her head through the open doorway.

I glance at the clock on the wall of the sorting room. "Yeah, tomorrow. But not until the afternoon."

"Good news." Her look of relief is almost comical, like it's her that'll be working on a Saturday and not me. "Well, I'm out of here. I'm heading home for my nephew's birthday this weekend, and the boss lady said I could peace out a few minutes early."

"Have fun. Eat some extra cake for me."

"Will do!" She laughs as she disappears.

I drum my fingers on the table, willing time to tick faster.

I got all the books put away already, so I've been sitting here doing my homework.

And by *doing my homework*, I really mean that I've been sitting here thinking about Maddox. Thinking about the game. Thinking about the way he looked in those tight football pants. Thinking about how many times he collided with other giant men on the field last night.

No wonder he didn't budge when I practically broke my nose on his chest.

I know I need to work on feeling good about my body.

It's a good body. It does what I need it to do. It's healthy. And I know I should appreciate it more. But I've always hated feeling so... *big*. So bulky and in the way.

But I don't feel that way around Maddox.

And maybe spending time around a giant man is a way to avoid my issues, but I don't care. I like feeling small in comparison.

My eyes lift back to the clock.

Five minutes to six is close enough to six.

The library itself will be open for another couple of hours, but only the front desk employees work until close.

Standing, I put my things away and straighten the room. Even though it's not messy, and I'll be the one who's in this room next since they don't need someone to reshelve books on a Saturday morning. But I still make sure everything is in order.

After a final check, I flick the light off and close the door behind me. Hiking my backpack up, I make my way through the back hallways.

I'm done with classes for the week. I'm caught up on home-work and free from responsibilities until I work again tomorrow afternoon. So why do I feel so... sad?

I squeeze my fingers around my backpack straps.

It's dumb to act like I don't know what my mood is about.

My sulky mood is the result of not seeing Maddox today.

And the fact that I probably won't see him tomorrow or Sunday.

And worse than all that, I'm fairly confident that by Monday, our little back and forth will be over.

My shoes scuff against the industrial carpet, and I look down at my outfit.

Black ballet flats. Dark wash jeans. And a black shirt with flowy half sleeves and a V-neck that's a little low for school but would be nice for a date.

I shake my head at myself.

I dressed for Maddox.

And I feel like a fool.

TWENTY-FOUR
MADDOX

FINALLY, Hannah steps out from the employee's-only area behind the main desk.

When I first got here, I spotted the back of her, the ends of her wavy locks brushing the center of her spine, just as she was walking off the main floor.

I didn't call out for her, figuring she'd be refilling her book cart and coming back out, but she didn't. And that was over an hour ago.

Closing my book, I push out of the armchair and move to cut her off.

My mouth opens to say her name, but then my throat goes dry.

Fuck me, I knew she had nice tits. But there's a difference between knowing and seeing.

Like she knows what I'm thinking, Hannah looks down at herself. But then I'm certain she doesn't know what I'm thinking, or how much I'm enjoying the view, because she shakes her head.

The only reason I'd shake my head over her cleavage is if my face was shoved in it.

And... Christ. She has freckles there too.

I clear my throat.

Hannah's head pops up, and her eyes widen when they see me.

"Maddox!" she says my name on a breathy gasp, and I feel it in my balls.

"Hey, Bunny."

Her cheeks blush like I knew they would, and I'm tempted to pound my fists against my chest. But instead, I act like a human and close the distance between us.

Hannah's eyes bounce around my body. Looking from my chest to my legs to my face. "Are you okay?"

I come to a stop before her. "Yes..." I drag the word out, not sure why I wouldn't be. "Are you okay?"

Her nose scrunches up. "What? No, I mean, are you okay, like physically?"

"Physically?" I repeat with a smirk.

She huffs. "From the game. When you banged yourself—"

I start to crack up. "I'm sorry, what did I do?"

She rolls her eyes even as she smiles. "You know what I mean."

The few people nearby look our way, and I swallow down my lingering laughter. I didn't mean to be so loud; this girl is just always catching me off guard.

She shifts her weight on her feet, and the movement draws my gaze down. "How's the ankle?"

"Hmm? Oh. Seriously, Maddox, it doesn't hurt at all. Not even a little."

I watch her face and accept that she's telling me the truth.

She lifts her brows like she's waiting for me to answer something.

"What?" I ask.

"Are you really okay?" She looks back at my chest. "I know you wear padding and stuff during the game, but still, some of those hits looked like they hurt."

Padding and stuff.

"God, you're cute." I say exactly what I'm thinking and enjoy the look of surprise on her face. "They're just called pads. And yeah, sometimes it hurts having a three-hundred-pound dude knock you to the ground, but I'm used to it."

TWENTY-FIVE

HANNAH

"BEING USED to it doesn't mean you're not injured," I point out while ignoring the *cute* comment.

Yes, being called cute is a compliment. But this is the guy I was thinking about while I touched myself last night. I don't want him to view me as *cute*. I want him to view me as... fuckable.

He spreads his arms wide and turns in a slow circle, giving me a view of all of him.

The move doesn't really prove his point. But fine, twist my arm, I'll look.

His jeans hug his thick thighs and ass. His gray T-shirt stretches across his massive body. And he's wearing a zip-up HOP U hoodie, which blocks my view of what I know are impressive back muscles, but it doesn't make him any less impressive to look at.

I'm pressing my lips together to keep myself from drooling.

Maddox lowers his arms when he's back to facing me. "See?"

"Okay, fine, you're not injured. But if you decide something hurts, I still have a can of pop in the fridge." I gesture toward the back room. "You can put it... wherever."

"Appreciate that." His smile is genuine. "What are you doing now?"

I notice all the people staring at us — or more like staring at *the* Mad Dog Maddox — and lower my voice. "Nothing. You?"

He lifts the book in his hand. I was too distracted looking at him to notice he was holding it.

"I was hoping to get some reading done. Thought the library would be a good place to do it."

"Oh." It's all I can think of saying in response.

"And since you said you liked it" — he gives the book a shake — "I thought you might be interested in joining me."

Oh!

"Sure," I answer without overthinking. "If you want the company."

Maybe I should've played it cooler than that? Pretended to have plans on a Friday night. But whatever. You only live once.

"Yeah?" His smile widens.

I nod.

I want to ask if he's inviting me as a friend or as *more*, but there's no good way to ask that. Not without making it incredibly awkward between us.

Then he holds out his hand. For me.

Slowly, with my heart stuttering inside my chest, I reach out and place my palm in his.

Maddox closes his large fingers around mine and turns us away from the central seating area toward the stairs.

I take a deep inhale through my nose.

We're holding hands.

I might be a bit naive, but I'm not *that* innocent. You don't walk around holding hands with someone you plan to friend zone.

Breathing evenly, I follow Maddox through a few rows of shelving.

When we reach the stairs, he breaks the silence. "I figured we could use one of the study rooms. I didn't bother signing one out since they're usually empty on a Friday night."

"You spend a lot of your Friday nights taking girls to the study rooms?"

He squeezes my hand with a chuckle. "You're my first."

I trip on the next step.

His deep laugh bounces around the stairwell as he raises our joined hands, helping me catch my balance.

"I meant you're the first girl I've asked to study with me. I'm not a..." He trails off.

Heat fills my face, and I keep my eyes forward.

"I'm not either," I practically whisper.

I don't know why it feels important to let him know I'm not a virgin.

Maybe it's because I don't want him to hold back around me. And if he thinks I'm *saving myself* for something, then he might.

He doesn't need to know it's only been once. And only when I was nineteen, and my best guy friend was moving across the country, and neither of us wanted to die a virgin. So we made a pact, and the night before he moved, we got drunk and had sex. The agreement was that we'd never talk to each other again because it would be too weird after. And the plan worked.

We gave each other our *V* cards. Neither of us remembers much of it, and we hugged out our hungover goodbyes and haven't talked since.

Truly, no regrets.

Maddox flexes his fingers around mine again, and the grunt he lets out sounds a little more gruff than any I've heard before.

We exit the stairwell on the second floor and walk toward the group of little rooms in the center of the building. There are eight study rooms situated in two rows of four.

They're small. Just big enough for a rectangular wooden table and four wooden chairs with scratchy blue seat cushions.

The handles don't lock, but there's a window on the top half of the door so you can see if it's occupied.

Maddox pulls me along, not stopping until we reach the room farthest from the stairs. The light is off, so we know it's empty.

As our steps slow, Maddox lets go of my hand to open the door but moves his other palm to the small of my back.

"After you." He applies a little extra pressure with his hand, and I step into the room.

Maddox turns the overhead light on as the door shuts, and I make my way around to the far side of the table.

But instead of sitting across from me, Maddox shuffles around the table from the other side and sits in the seat next to mine.

TWENTY-SIX
MADDOX

HANNAH TRIES NOT TO REACT, but I know she wasn't expecting me to sit beside her.

I set my book on the table, watching her eyes move from the book up to my face.

"Do you have anything else?" She glances at her backpack sitting on the table in front of her, pulling out a thing of orange Tic Tac's and offering me one.

I shake my head as I pop a few into my mouth. "The assignment isn't due until the end of the semester, and my memory is good. I'm just a really slow reader." I lift a shoulder, for some reason not feeling self-conscious over admitting that to her.

I'm not stupid. I'm just not a fast reader.

It took me a while to separate those two things in my mind. Mostly because of the shit other students would say. But even though I know I'll never be the type of person who can read a book in a day, I still enjoy reading.

Hannah picks up *The Count of Monte Cristo*. "Are you sure there wasn't a longer book to choose from?"

I grin.

This right here is why I feel so comfortable around her.

No jokes about me being some dumb jock.

No pitying remarks.

Just acceptance.

"I'll be honest, I didn't know how many pages there were when I chose it," I admit. "But the other options didn't interest me, or I'd already seen the movie."

Since we're sitting side by side, Hannah has to tip her head back to look at me.

She lifts her pointer finger. "First, it's a freaking awesome movie. Highly recommend." She lifts a second finger. "What sort of assignment is this?"

I turn to face her better and hold up two fingers. "We need to read a book, watch the movie adaptation, then write a report on why the book is better."

"Seriously?" Hannah laughs, causing me to smile.

"Okay, so the teacher said to write about which version has better storytelling, but her bias was pretty obvious." I lower one of my fingers, counting down Hannah's points. "How about when I finish the book, you and I watch the movie together?"

Hannah gives me a little nod. "I'd like that." She taps her nail against the cover of the book. "Do you have a girlfriend?"

I snort before I can stop myself. "Sorry." I grab her hand before she can pull away. "I'm not laughing at you. Just..." I shake my head. "I wouldn't be sitting here, with you, in this tiny room, if I had a girlfriend. Just like if I were your boyfriend, you wouldn't be sitting in one of these rooms with someone else." I brush my thumb across the inside of her wrist. "You don't have a boyfriend, right?"

Her pulse is strong against my touch as she shakes her head. "No. No boyfriend."

"Good."

She gives me a half smile before blowing out a puff of air.

"Sorry, I didn't mean to sound like I was accusing you or anything. I just saw someone with a sign about you at the game yesterday and..." She shrugs.

"Did the sign say *I'm Mad Dog's girlfriend?*"

Her lips pull to the side. "No, but that's probably a good way to get free drinks."

I chuckle. "Men are pretty simple. It'd probably work."

"Next time."

I know she's joking along with me, but I like hearing her say that. *Next time.*

"How would you like to do this?" She pushes her bag farther across the table, making space in front of herself.

A vision of lifting her onto the surface, spreading her legs, and plunging into her flashes into my mind.

I almost groan.

On the stairs, when she said *I'm not either,* I was torn between wanting to spank her for not waiting for me and wanting to beat the other man into the ground for touching what was obviously meant to be mine.

It's hypocritical to want her to never have seen another dick before. Because I've, well... But it doesn't matter what either of us has done in the past. That's the past. Now is now.

"Maddox?"

I blink. "I'm good. Just... thinking."

Thinking I need to adjust my half-hard cock, but I can't really do that subtly.

Her brows knit together. "Are you sure you're okay? I don't know how you can play like that and still walk after the game."

"You that worried about me, Bunny?"

She heaves out a breath. "I just find it hard to believe you aren't covered in bruises. If I got hit like that, I'd lie on the floor crying."

I turn until I'm completely sideways in my chair, facing

her. "If anyone ever hit you, they'd be the one lying on the floor crying." Her eyes widen, and I roll my shoulders out. "Remember, you asked for this."

"What—"

Before she can finish her question, I reach down and pull up the hem of my shirt, lifting it up to my chest.

"Maddox!" Hannah gasps, glancing at the window like she's worried someone else might see.

"I'm just showing you that I'm fine." I lift my shirt higher.

"You — um..." Her eyes burn a trail of heat across my skin. She looks everywhere.

I'm too big to be shredded. I don't have a defined six-pack like some of the guys do.

But I'm all strength. Thick. Built for power.

I need to be huge. If I wasn't, I wouldn't be on the team.

A soft hand presses against my pec, and I clench my jaw.

"Wow." I don't think she means to say it. But she does.

I flex, causing my chest muscles to expand under her touch.

Her eyes snap up to meet mine.

"Believe me now?" I ask, my voice deeper than normal.

Hannah swallows. "Yeah." Then she looks back down at my body.

Like she's just realizing what she's doing, she snatches her hand back.

This isn't the first time she's touched me. But it's the first time it was skin on skin. And I want more.

She scoots back in her chair, her cheeks blooming a deep red. "I'm sorry. I didn't — I shouldn't have touched you like that."

"You can touch me any way you want." I lift my shirt higher and wiggle my eyebrows. I don't want her to feel like she did anything wrong.

Her mouth pinches like she's trying not to laugh, even as she looks back toward the window.

"Going once..." I lower and raise my shirt.

"Oh my god, put your shirt down!" She finally breaks, laughing.

I lift it higher, twisting side to side, making sure she can see as much as she wants to.

"Maddox." She leans forward, reaching for my shirt.

We're facing each other, our sides against the backs of our chairs, our knees touching.

And when she gets back within touching distance, arms outstretched toward me, I let go of my shirt. And I reach for her.

TWENTY-SEVEN
HANNAH

AS MY FINGERS brush the fabric of the T-shirt, his hands move, and he grips me under my arms.

I don't have time to react before he drags me forward. And pulls me off my chair and onto his lap.

Or, more specifically, to straddle his lap.

When he lifted me, my traitorous legs spread themselves.

I flatten my palms against his chest, where I was touching him before, only this time it's rising and falling with heavy breaths.

He slides his hands down my sides and grips my hips.

"Mr. Lovelace," I whisper. "What are you doing?"

His lids half lower when I say his name like that, and the thighs beneath my butt flex.

"Fuck, Babe. I'm gonna need you to call me that again." Maddox's voice is nearly a growl. "And I'm gonna need you to be in a skirt when you do it."

Warmth floods my core, a pulse building between my legs.

This is crazy.

Ridiculous.

A dream.

I lean forward. "Why a skirt?"

He drags my body closer. "All the better to fuck you in."

His growled words startle a gasp out of me. I was not expecting him to be so direct.

A strong hand slides up my back, holding me in place as Maddox closes the distance between us and presses his mouth to mine.

I don't even try to resist.

His lips are warm and surprisingly soft.

Demanding but gentle.

I tilt my head, getting closer, as I slide my hands up his chest and wrap my arms around his neck.

The movement causes a groan to roll out of Maddox's throat, and he uses his hold on me to pull me in even closer.

And that's when I feel it. Against the front of my jeans.

A shiver of desire rolls through me.

I felt it the other day. Felt his hardness against my belly when he was holding me. But having it between my legs. Having it there. Lined up where I want him most.

It's intoxicating.

He's intoxicating.

His tongue swipes across the seam of my mouth, and I open, letting him in.

And when he tastes me, my hips rock.

This time, we both groan.

All of him, every damn inch, is big.

So freaking big.

The kiss deepens. Grows. Becomes more frantic.

We lean into each other, and his facial hair rasps at the edges of my mouth.

Just like I imagined.

I want to touch more of him.

Want to feel the warmth of his body again.

I move my hand from his neck, down his chest, then over the hem of his shirt that's still bunched up over his stomach, then farther until I have his warm skin under my palm.

His tongue pulls out of my mouth, and mine chases it, swiping against his lips.

Behind me, his knees lift, and I slide a little more down his thighs. Our bodies are flush now. And the pressure is there. Right where I want him. Where I need him.

"You're a bad girl, Miss Utley."

I curl my fingers, dragging my nails across his flesh. "I have no idea what you're talking about, Mr. Lovelace."

A big palm grips my ass. And god, it feels so good.

He makes me feel so good.

A burst of loud laughter filters through the door, reminding us that we're not alone.

Maddox drops his forehead to my shoulder.

I lift the hand from his stomach and hook my arm back around his neck, hugging him to me, as we both catch our breath.

The hand still on my ass flexes. "Fucking hell, Hannah."

A puff of humor leaves me. Glad he seems to be as affected as I am. "You started it."

He snorts and shakes his head against me.

Giving in to the urge I've had since I first saw him, I slide one of my hands up the back of his neck and run my fingers through his short dark hair.

He nuzzles into my touch.

I want to stay like this forever, but the reminder of other people also serves as a reminder that this is where I work. And I can't get fired for fooling around in a study room.

I rub my fingers through his hair once more. "So, *The Count of Monte Cristo?*"

His back rises with a deep inhale. "*The* fucking *Count of Monte Cristo.*"

Maddox lifts his head, and his hooded gaze fills me with confidence.

I force a serious expression onto my face. "Upon closer inspection, I've come to the conclusion that your body is satisfactory."

He fights a smirk. "I appreciate the thorough checkup, Dr. Utley."

I press my lips together and nod. "My pleasure." I reach for his shirt and tug it down, covering his tempting middle. "But I'll still have to submit the bill to your insurance. Following protocol and all that."

"I understand." Maddox holds a steady look before he chuckles and shakes his head. "You're something else, Little Bunny."

"Something good, I hope."

"The best."

Sparks of joy dance across my skin.

Strong hands rest against my sides. "But if I fail this class, I'm blaming you."

"Can't have that."

I try to climb off his lap, but my feet are hanging above the ground.

I wiggle my hips. "Mind giving me a hand?"

He lets go of me with one hand, then smacks it down against my ass. The spank is loud in the little room.

"Mr. Lovelace!"

Maddox is grinning as he rubs his palm against my butt. "Sorry, but I've wanted to do that since the first time you ran away from me."

"Brute," I accuse without heat.

Sighing, he grips my waist with both hands and slides me

backward. One of his legs moves beneath me while he uses his foot to hook the leg of my chair, dragging it over so I go right from being on his legs onto the seat.

Unable to help myself, my gaze drops to his lap.

The tent in his jeans has my heartbeat picking back up.

He presses his palm down on his length and groans. "You gotta stop looking at it like that."

I bite my lip. "Sorry."

"No, you're not," he laughs. "But you can make up for the torment by reading to me."

Turning toward the table, I clear my throat and put my hand on the book, dragging it over in front of me.

"Where are you?" I ask when I don't see a bookmark.

"Page one." I can hear the smile in his voice, and I'm not sure if he's lying, but I decide we might as well start together at the beginning.

Opening the cover, I watch out the corner of my eye as he scoots his chair closer. And closer. Until it's right up against mine.

It's been a long time since I've read aloud to someone, but I don't feel nervous. Maddox won't judge me if I mispronounce a word.

He settles his arm across the back of my chair, his chin going to my shoulder as he leans into my side.

"I'm ready." His voice rumbles directly from his chest into my body.

Relaxing into him, I prop the book on the table and read the first line.

"On February twenty-fourth..."

TWENTY-EIGHT
MADDOX

THE WAY she reads is almost lyrical.

Her soft voice rises and falls with the emotions in the words. She makes it a... production.

The chapters have melded together, the story coming to life through her telling of it. And I know I won't be able to read the rest of the book alone. I'm going to need her to do this with me every week. Hell, every day.

Hannah turns the page, and I slide my eyes away from the words on the paper and focus on her hand.

The way it cradles the book.

The way she slowly slides her thumb down the edge of the page, tracking her progress.

Then I think about the way her fingers felt in my hair. On my chest. Pressing against my bare stomach.

My dick twitches in my jeans.

To be fair to my dick, he's been dying for attention since I pulled her onto my lap. Since he felt the heat of her. But he'll have to wait a bit longer.

I tip my head to the side and rub my cheek against her shoulder.

Her huff of laughter causes me to smile. And sitting here, in the library study room, I wonder if maybe this is it. If I've found my girl. My ride or die.

She keeps reading, but my mind moves away from the wronged sailor to my future.

I want to play pro ball.

I want to make my family proud.

I want my little brother, Maximus, the six-year-old terror, to be able to count on me. And I want him to keep telling everyone that when he grows up, he'll be the quarterback on my team — even though I'll probably be retired by then.

And I want to do all of those things with a partner at my side.

A woman.

Hannah turns another page.

Maybe *this* woman.

The light in the room changes, and Hannah's shoulder shifts beneath my cheek as she lifts her head to look out the window.

My brows knit. "Why'd the lights go off?"

It's still bright in the study room, but the lights beyond our little space have gone out.

"I think they're on timers, not sensors," Hannah answers. "So they shouldn't... Oh, shit."

I lift my head. "What?"

Hannah keeps staring out the window. "What time is it?"

With my left arm draped around Hannah's shoulders, I bend my elbow and twist my wrist so we can both read my watch.

Ten thirty.

"I didn't realize it was so late." I roll out my shoulders. "Do you have to get going somewhere?"

Slowly, Hannah turns her face to look up at me.

"It's ten thirty." Her eyes are wide.

"What happens at ten thirty?" I glance back at the darkened window.

"Nothing. But the library closed at ten."

TWENTY-NINE
HANNAH

I SHUT the book and shove it into my backpack. "Come on."

Maddox stands at the same time I do, taking the bag from my hands before I can put it on. He slings it over his shoulder and follows me out into the main part of the library.

All the overhead lights are off, and it's dark, but the moon outside sends just enough light through the windows to illuminate our way.

The library is always quiet, but this is different. And when the study room door slams behind us, it makes me jump.

Maddox drapes his arm around my shoulders as he moves to walk next to me. "Don't worry, I'll protect you from the ghost."

I'm pretty sure he's teasing me. But...

I glance up at him. "There's not really a ghost, is there?"

Maddox pulls me into his side. "I'm just kidding. It's in one of the science buildings."

"Not funny." I try to keep the smile out of my voice.

Since the lights are always on during business hours, I

haven't paid attention to any light switches. So I'm not going to bother looking for them now.

Together, we make our way to the stairs.

The stairwell is lit with a red Exit sign, so we can see the steps as we take them down, but the darkness waiting for us on the first floor tells me all I need to know.

Everyone is gone.

"Huh." Maddox doesn't sound concerned.

He dropped his arm from around my shoulders on the stairs, and I feel his fingers brush mine.

They brush mine a second time, and I know it's not an accident.

Turning my wrist, I let our palms meet, and Maddox wraps his fingers around mine.

Our steps are quiet on the carpet as we cut between the low shelves and seating areas toward the front doors. The entryway is four doors across, all made of glass, with a small vestibule beyond — home to the vending machine — then there's another row of glass doors that leads outside.

Moonlight illuminates the entrance, but the lights there are off too.

A mixture of anxiety and excitement zings through me as we close the distance.

And when Maddox stretches his free hand out, I hold my breath.

His palm connects with the door, and he pushes.

But it doesn't budge.

Because we've been locked in.

THIRTY
MADDOX

NEXT TO ME, Hannah reaches out with the hand I'm not holding and tries the other door.

It doesn't move.

There are two more doors, so we sidestep over and try them.

Nothing.

There has to be another exit, a back door, but if these are closed and the lights are off and no one else is here... Then those doors are locked too.

I flex my fingers around Hannah's as we look through the panes of glass. There's no one.

No wandering students.

No custodial staff.

No security guards in sight.

Just an empty campus.

And us. Alone in the library.

Heat travels up my spine, building in my chest, and I turn to face Hannah.

THIRTY-ONE

HANNAH

MADDOX TURNS BESIDE ME.

It's just us.

No one else.

No one to catch us or see us.

Swallowing, I press my palm against the cool glass of the door. "We could try to call someone."

"We could." His voice is low. Gruff.

"But I don't know who to call," I whisper.

"Me either." Maddox traces his thumb across the back of my hand.

"Or..." I let the possibilities hang in the air, swirling with the tension between us.

"I like *or*," Maddox says as he tugs on my arm.

I spin with the movement, turning to face him. And I let go.

I let go of my inhibitions.

I let go of the worry that this is all a dream.

I let go of his hand and throw my arms around his neck.

Maddox crashes into me. And it reminds me of watching him play yesterday. His big, powerful body full of so much strength and control. But he doesn't bowl me over. The only destruction he causes tonight is to my senses. To my equilibrium. Throwing my world off balance as his big hands grip my ass and he lifts me into the air.

There's no time to think anymore when his mouth finds mine.

My lips part for him as my legs wrap around his waist.

He's so thick, so big, I can't hook my feet together behind him, so I just dig my heels into his lower back, and his grip on me holds me up.

"Hannah. Fuck," he pants into my mouth.

I consume his words, clawing at the back of his neck, trying to get him closer.

A growl rumbles through his chest, and he uses his grip on my ass to pull me tighter against him. Against the hardness between my legs.

I whimper.

I don't mean to.

I just can't stop myself.

He just feels so damn good.

Kissing him earlier was just the start. *This*. This is different.

He groans, rolling his hips against me but never pulling his mouth from mine.

He tastes like the orange Tic Tacs we shared in the study room.

He feels like the strongest man in the world.

He makes me want more.

I pull my mouth away from his, my lips already swollen, to tell him I want more.

But I'm breathing too heavily to speak.

And he's already walking.

He slides his hands lower until he's holding me at the very

tops of my thighs, right at the bottom curve of my ass, his fingertips so close to my center.

I curl my hips forward, pressing myself into his length.

"Fuck." He shifts me up an inch, then back down.

The friction makes us both groan.

"Maddox," I breathe out.

"I know, Babe." He presses his lips to mine. "I'll take care of
it." Another kiss.

His words pull a moan out of my throat, and I curl my hips
in again.

I want that. I want that so badly.

My tongue slides out across his lower lip, and he stumbles,
bumping into something in the hazy dark.

"Shit," he chuckles. Then he groans as he does that lifting
thing again, rubbing me against his dick. "You're gonna be the
death of me."

I pull my mouth away from his and lower my head so I can
kiss along the side of his neck and he can see where he's going.

I press soft kisses to his throat, feeling the heavy pulse
against my lips.

"Goddamn."

I kiss again.

We tilt, and I cling tighter, trusting him not to drop me.

I can hear furniture being moved, and I imagine him
balancing us on one leg as he kicks things into place.

Lifting my head, I see we're in the back corner in one of the
reading areas, far enough away from the entrance that if
someone did come in, they wouldn't be able to see us.

We shift again, followed by wood knocking together, and I
look down.

At a bed.

I almost laugh.

It's not a bed, per se. But Maddox has kicked a trio of

benches together, their wood legs perfectly lined up and their padded blue tops making a small but comfortable-enough-looking surface.

Maddox sees where I'm looking and stills, our chests heaving against each other.

"Sorry. I... We don't have to."

I turn my head back to meet his eyes. "Maddox, I want to."

Even in the dim light, I can see his jaw flex. "Thank fuck."

I don't have time to smile before his mouth is back on mine.

He lowers us, and my butt hits the first bench. Then I'm lying back across the second bench, and finally, the third acts as my pillow.

Maddox lifts off me, looking down. "This won't work."

A flicker of rejection burns in my chest, but he douses it with his next words.

"I need to see you." He grips my shoulders and pulls me up to a sitting position.

His hands close around the bottom of my shirt, and he pulls it up over my head.

My hair falls around my face, and I'm brushing it back when his hands are on my bra.

They search for just a second before releasing the hooks.

I refuse to think about how many times he's done that to be so good at it.

Maddox pulls the bra from my body and tosses it aside.

"Jesus," he moans.

Then he's palming my breasts, and I'm the one moaning.

I grab his forearms, steadying myself.

He kneels on the floor before me and leans forward.

My fingers curl, my nails cutting into his skin as he takes one of my nipples into his mouth.

The sensation is... all-consuming.

His mouth is so hot against my pebbled flesh that it pulls the air out of my lungs.

He curses, then moves to the other peak and sucks it into his mouth.

That one time I had sex before... it wasn't like this.

Maddox releases my breast, then licks a line up my chest. "These fucking freckles. They taste like sunshine."

Fingers pinch at my nipples, and I moan.

"Lie back." Maddox lets go of my breasts and pushes me back with a hand on my side and shoulder.

He stands then, looming over me, looking larger than life, as he sheds his hoodie, then pulls his shirt off.

I start to sit up, wanting to reach for him.

"Stay still, Little Bunny."

I do as he says. But then my mouth drops open when he undoes his jeans and pushes them down his thighs.

He's wearing boxers. But they are doing nothing to hide his size.

He reaches into them, and though I can't see the details, I know he's wrapping his fingers around his dick.

The fabric stretches as he adjusts his position, and then...

I lick my lips.

The head of his cock is sticking out the top band of his boxers, the elastic keeping it against his stomach.

I start to sit up again. The urge to put that thing in my mouth is too strong to ignore.

But he moves before I can, dropping back to his knees.

His hands move to my waist and undo the button on my jeans, then the zipper.

"Hips up."

I lift my feet so they're on the edge of the bench and do as he asks.

Unlike for himself, Maddox doesn't leave my underwear

on. He pulls them off with my jeans, only pausing to tug my shoes off as well before he throws the whole bundle on top of my bra.

I've never been completely naked like this in front of anybody. But right now, I don't even care. With Maddox looking at me like that, there's not a single part of me that's self-conscious.

Warm hands press my thighs open, and I expect him to get up again. Expect him to push his boxers off. But he doesn't.

He leans in.

THIRTY-TWO

MADDOX

I FLATTEN my tongue against her slit and lick.

My moan is immediate, and Hannah nearly arches off the bench.

She tastes so fucking good. So fucking delicious.

"So fucking wet," I murmur.

I curl my arm around her thigh, holding her in place, and lap at her again. With my other hand, I reach up to play with her amazing tits. Her nipples feel perfect between my fingers.

She tugs at my hair with both hands, pulling on the short strands. "Mad — what are you — fuck —"

I let her pull my head back a few inches. "I know you said we're not supposed to eat in the library." Holding her gaze, I lick the shine off my lips. "But we're breaking the rules tonight."

I spread her legs wider and lower my mouth.

"No one—"

I smile against her pussy as her words get cut off in a gasp.

That's right, Hannah. Real men eat pussy.

Closing my lips around her clit, I suck and flick my tongue over the little bundle of nerves.

"Oh my god." Her pants are becoming ragged. And I release her clit to swipe my tongue up the length of her again.

"That's it," I coax her as I tease her flesh. "Come on my face like a good girl."

I want to tell her to forget about her past boyfriends. That I'll fuck them right out of her memory. But I don't want her thinking about them at all.

Not now. Not ever again.

She starts to tremble.

Tightening my arm around her leg, I move my other hand.

My tongue works her clit — jiggling it — as I slide one finger up and down her slit.

She's fucking soaked.

And I need to feel more of her heat.

I push my fingertip inside her.

She jolts. Her body arches.

If she hadn't told me otherwise, I'd swear she was untouched.

"Let go, Babe. Show me how you feel."

I suck her clit, just as I shove my finger all the way inside her, and she bursts.

Her channel clamps down, and her body convulses as she comes.

It's so hot.

And I can't wait anymore.

Sitting back, I pull my pants free from the pile of clothing and take the condom out of my wallet.

Hannah's still breathing heavily, but she lifts her head to watch me.

I catch her eye before I tear the package open. "I'm not a player. And I didn't expect to do this tonight. I just—"

"Maddox." She cuts me off. "Shut up and take your boxers off."

I grin.

Goddamn, I like this girl.

Biting the corner of the condom wrapper, I leave it between my teeth, then stand.

If she wants to see me, then she'll see all of me.

With both hands, I push my boxers down.

THIRTY-THREE
HANNAH

MY STOMACH FLIPS when Maddox frees his cock.

It's long. And thick. And honestly, in comparison, I might as well be a virgin, because it's twice as big as the one I've experienced before.

Maddox closes one fist around his length and slides it up and down. "Keep those legs open for me, Bunny."

My knees had started to close of their own accord, suddenly worried for my health.

"That's, um." I nod to his dick. "Big."

He chuckles a second before I hear the condom wrapper tear. "And you're gonna take all of it."

My heart — which had just started to recover — picks up speed again.

He rolls the thin layer of protection down his length.

I'm on the pill, but I'm glad he came prepared. Because this man, and that cock, could easily have me making stupid decisions.

Maddox grips my knees and pushes them up and out, opening me farther.

Then he climbs up and kneels on the bench.

"Fuck, Babe. I already know your pussy is going to feel amazing." He rests one hand against my inner thigh while the other grips his dick. He runs the tip up and down my entrance. "Ready?"

I nod.

"Tell me, Hannah. Let me hear it."

The cool air of the library skitters over my exposed skin, but I still feel like I'm burning up. Like I'm on fire.

I fist my hands at my sides. "I'm ready."

Then he's pushing forward.

And I wasn't ready.

I stretch around him.

He groans above me.

My eyes close.

And he shoves the rest of the way in.

My mouth opens. To scream or moan, I don't know. And I'll never know because then he's there.

Maddox is over me.

Elbows planted beside my head.

His mouth on mine.

His lips sealing in my sounds.

His hips thrusting.

His cock sliding out, then pushing in.

And it's so much.

It's too much.

My legs wind around his waist. And my hands claw at his sides.

And... fuck. I can't even think anymore.

"That's it," he grunts. "So tight." He slams in harder. "Taking me so good." He kisses me again.

My nipples scrape against his chest hair as he moves above me, sending new sparks of desire straight to my center.

"Maddox," I pant. "Oh god," I cry.

And he doesn't stop.

Doesn't stop moving.

Doesn't stop filling me.

And then he shifts his body *higher* over me. So when he slides in and out, the base of his cock rubs against my clit. My already overworked clit.

I tilt my hips into the feeling.

"Open your eyes."

My body does as commanded.

His beautiful dark eyes are hovering above me.

"Tell me how you feel," he demands.

"Good," I answer automatically, then lift my hips to match his. "Feels so good."

He rolls his hips, getting deeper than before, and I arch my neck.

"So full." I dig my fingers into his sides. "I feel so full."

"Fuck." Maddox drops his mouth to mine.

His tongue swipes into my mouth. His body presses against my nipples. And his cock grinds into my clit.

And I break.

"That's it." Maddox pulls back to watch me.

My cries aren't swallowed this time. They're loud. Echoing through the stacks.

"That's fucking it."

He thrusts once more.

Pushes deep once more.

Then he's coming with me.

His groan is as loud as my cries were, and they sound like heaven.

His cock throbs inside me, and my body tenses around him. My pussy is contracting so hard a sound of distress leaves my body.

Maddox throws his head back, and I drag my hands over his muscles as they flex.

He's the most handsome man I've ever seen.

And right now, he's all mine.

102

THIRTY-FOUR
MADDOX

MY LIMBS SHAKE as I do my best not to collapse my full weight onto Hannah.

"Just need a moment." I say the words into her hair.

She slides her smooth hands up and down my sides. "Take your time."

I force my lungs to fill. "I'll get up as soon as my soul reenters my body."

Hannah laughs, and it makes her pussy squeeze my still-hard cock.

I groan.

"Sorry!" she laughs again, and the sound is... perfect.

I don't know how she does it. But with her, I get to experience everything.

The heat of desire.

The calmness of just being near each other.

The lightness of laughter, even in a moment like this.

"You're fucking perfection." I sigh.

I should feel regret, blurting that out, but I don't.

And when Hannah lets out a contented hum, I know it was the right thing to say.

"You're pretty great yourself, Maddox Lovelace."

In the dark, with my expression hidden in her neck, I smile.

THIRTY-FIVE

HANNAH

WALKING BACK FROM THE BATHROOM — which was thankfully lit with the same red Exit sign as the stairwell — I press my lips together, wanting to keep the dopey smile off my face.

I'm not trying to play it cool or pretend that what we just did wasn't the best experience of my life, but I don't need to look like I'm completely in love.

Even though I might be.

I push that thought aside and settle for smitten.

As I round the corner, I find Maddox shoving even more furniture together.

Definitely smitten.

"What are you building now?" I come to a stop next to him, both of us dressed again.

He gestures to the four armchairs he wedged against the four corners of the bench bed. "I don't know how much you move around in your sleep, but I don't really want the benches sliding apart and us crashing to the floor."

"I'll have you know; I sleep completely still. Like a lady."

Maddox snorts. "Sure you do. But on the off chance you don't, these will hopefully work. And those." He points to the cushions on the far end of the little bed. "Are our pillows."

I glance at the chairs and see the missing back cushions. "Clever."

He looks down at me. "I figured those were safer than the butt cushions. But either way" — he pats his chest — "you can use me as your pillow."

I bat my eyes at him. "My hero."

He surprises me by dropping his mouth to mine and pressing a quick kiss on my lips.

Then he makes up for the sweetness by slapping my ass. "Now get in bed."

Crawling across the benches, I decide not to ask about his roommates.

I'm new here and haven't had time to make friends, so I don't have anyone to call. But Maddox has been here for years. He knows everyone. He lives in the Football House with several of his teammates — a tidbit of information I got from Sissy earlier today. Not that his roommates can unlock the doors for us, but they could fan out around campus and find a security guard. They could do something. But for whatever reason, Maddox isn't calling them.

And I'm okay with it.

Maddox lies down beside me, spreading his arm wide and patting his chest.

I'm super okay with it.

I shuffle over, pressing my front into his side, and rest my head on that spot right where his shoulder and chest meet.

Using his far hand, he lifts his unzipped hoodie. "Our blanket."

I help him lay it over our top halves.

With our *blanket* in place, Maddox curls his hand around my side, holding me to him.

"Comfy?" He yawns.

"Mm-hmm." Inhaling, I let my lungs fill with his scent, then I hook my knee up over his leg, and something sharp pokes me through his jeans.

I slide my hand down between us and slip my fingers into his pocket.

Maddox twists his hips, giving me space, and I'm able to grab the item.

I hold it up, tipping my head back to look at him. "Really?"

His smile is sleepy. And incredibly adorable.

"Here." He takes it from me and presses one corner of the triangle between his pecs with his pointer finger against the opposite corner, propping the paper football upright. "Make a wish."

I can't stop my grin. "I think that's for birthdays."

He shrugs the shoulder my head is on. "Same rules apply for finger football as for birthday cakes."

"How silly of me not to know that." I settle my cheek back into its spot.

"I live to teach." He presses his lips against the top of my head. "Now make a wish and flick it."

I battle the butterflies in my stomach and focus on the task. "What am I aiming for?"

He makes a contemplative sound.

"Gotta land it on that chair for it to come true." He uses his shoeless foot to point at the chair securing the far corner of our bench bed.

I rest my hand just behind the football, the edge of my palm against his chest.

Then I close my eyes and make my wish.

I wish for Maddox Lovelace to be the man I marry.

THIRTY-SIX
MADDOX

HANNAH'S FLICK connects with the edge of the paper football, sending it flying.

It spins through the air, end over end, toward the chair.

I lift my head to watch it.

When it starts to veer off course, I kick up my foot and help it, causing the triangle to land on the chair.

THIRTY-SEVEN
HANNAH – SATURDAY

"BUNNY."

The whispered word has my eyes blinking open. And I'm greeted with sunlight.

It's faint. Early morning. But it's light.

"Morning." My voice is quiet and scratchy.

"Morning," Maddox says back. He sounds just as sleepy.

I start to lift my head, then groan, my body protesting the movement.

The shoulder under my head shakes as Maddox laughs. "I know. I feel like every joint I have is going to crack as soon as I try to move."

"I can't believe we actually slept here all night." I stretch out my top leg, realizing neither of us moved an inch.

Maddox lifts his watch hand. "A solid five hours."

A disgruntled sound comes out of me, causing him to chuckle.

"I know, Babe. Not nearly enough time together." He tightens his arm around me.

I snort. "Well, I don't know about you, but I'm going back to sleep as soon as we find our way out of here."

"Speaking of." Maddox points his toes and stretches his legs. "We should probably dismantle our base camp before anyone finds us."

"Agreed. I have to be back here to work this afternoon, and I'd rather not have everyone talking about us."

Maddox groans, then he rolls away from me. All the way off the edge of the benches, thumping onto the floor.

"Oh my god," I laugh and scramble after him. "Are you okay?"

Shaking his head, he climbs up to stand. "Meant to do that."

I press my lips together and nod. "It was real smooth."

He rolls his shoulders out with a wince. "I am impressive."

My eyes drop to the front of his jeans. He left them undone while we slept, and they're doing nothing to hide his bulge.

"Like I said." He reaches down to zip up.

I roll my eyes, but he's right. He's impressive everywhere.

Maddox bends down and picks my bra up off the floor. Sleeping in jeans was bad enough, no way was I wearing an underwire to bed.

"Want to go put this on while I put the furniture away?"

I fight the urge to blush. Maddox holding my bra is hardly the most personal thing we did over the past twenty-four hours.

"Yes, please." I climb off our bench bed, bringing the hoodie with me.

Before I can grab the bra, Maddox lifts it out of reach.

My eyes follow the movement, my head tipping back, and he uses the angle to tip his face forward and kiss me.

His lips are firm against mine.

It's just one kiss.

A simple press.

But it feels like so much more.

He pulls back. "If we do that any longer, I'm going to want to put these benches to use again."

I dart my hand up and grab my bra. "Maybe we can use an actual bed next time."

Too late, I realize what I just said. But instead of looking smothered, Maddox looks smug.

"Agreed."

Before I can get us both in trouble, I hurry to the bathroom.

I return two minutes later, wearing my bra and his hoodie, and while Maddox straightens the last cushion, I slip my backpack onto my shoulders.

With everything in place, I take his outstretched hand, and we walk toward the front entrance.

The silence between us is... comfortable. Familiar.

Our steps slow as we reach the doors.

"Any ideas on how..." Maddox trails off as we watch an older man in a jumpsuit approach the doors from the other side, pushing a custodial cart. "Well, that was easy."

The man unlocks the outer door and is halfway through the vestibule before he notices us.

He jerks to a stop, eyes widening.

Maddox lifts his hand and projects his voice. "Morning!"

"Morning," he says back, sounding confused. Then he narrows his eyes on Maddox's face and points at him. "Aren't you the Mad Dog boy?" His voice is muffled through the glass.

Maddox grins. "That's me."

"That was a good scoop and score on Thursday. Fun to watch."

"Appreciate that. It was fun to do." Maddox gestures to the door. "Mind letting me and my girl out of here? We lost track of time studying and got locked in last night."

My girl. Gah.

The man lifts the keys. "You mind signing something for me?"

Maddox laughs. "Yeah, man. I sign it, and you pretend this never happened. Deal?"

"Deal." The man nods and unlocks the door.

Notebook signed, Maddox and I walk out into the fresh morning air.

We stop and turn to face each other.

"I'd like to do that again." Maddox searches my gaze. "And not just the naked part. Everything that happened before it too."

I bite my lip, his words filling me with a lightness I didn't know I needed.

"I'd like that, too," I tell him.

Maddox takes a step closer. "After your shift?"

"Today?"

He nods. "I can't wait longer than that."

"Today." I breathe my agreement.

He leans down. "Promise?"

I set my free hand to his chest, lifting onto my tiptoes.

"Promise." I whisper the word against his lips.

To be continued in Love, Utley

Order Dear Rosie, book 2 in the Love Letters series, now!

ABOUT THE AUTHOR

S.J. Tilly was born and raised in Minnesota, which is why so many of her books are based there. But she now resides in the beautiful mountains of Colorado with her husband and misfit herd of rescue boxers.

When she's not busy writing a new book, she can be found plotting her next book...

To stay up to date on all things Tilly, make sure to follow her on her socials, join her newsletter, and interact whenever you feel like it! Links to everything on her website sjtilly.com

ACKNOWLEDGMENTS

Keeping this short, sweet, and unedited - because I somehow deleted my previous acknowledgments... whoops!

Thank you to my people. My mom. My Kerissa. My sprint group. My BeanBaggers and Banshees and ARC readers.

I love you.

I love my job.

And I hope you love the Love Letters Series.

Xoxo

BOOKS BY THIS AUTHOR

Love Letters Series

Contemporary Romance

Tackled in the Stacks

I caught her staring at me from across the quad, eyes fixed on the football jersey stretched across my wide chest. And if I flexed my muscles, showing off the strength of a defensive tackle, it was just to see her blush.

And then she did, and I couldn't get her out of my mind.

Her wide eyes. The freckles on her cheeks.

I needed to know her. The girl who scampered away every time we bumped into each other—by accident and by design. The girl who shyly agreed to come to my game, getting her first taste of football. The girl, Hannah Utley, who worked at the campus library and let me rest my head on her shoulder as she read to me in one of the study rooms.

It was innocent. Mostly.

Until we lose track of time and discover that the library has closed. And we're locked inside.

Now it's me and Hannah in the stacks.

Alone.

With nothing but desire between us.

Love, Utley

Hannah

Maddox Lovelace. The captivating football player I met in college.

The one I only knew for a week. A week that was... life-changing.

Until my phone rang, and I had no choice but to go home.

I left Maddox a letter, putting my feelings on paper, giving him my number, hoping he'd call.

But he didn't call.

He never called.

He got drafted into the professional league and lived like a king while I stayed home and struggled to stay afloat.

I may have followed his career, but now that he's retired from football, I've forced myself to stop thinking about him.

And it's okay that I won't ever see him again. That week in college was fifteen years ago.

I'm not in love with Maddox anymore.

I might even hate him.

Maddox

Hannah Utley. The name that's haunted me since my senior year of college.

The girl who caught my attention with her wide eyes and freckled nose.

Who spent one week twisting up my insides until she stole a piece of my heart the night we got locked inside the campus library.

The girl who disappeared without a word.

It's the name of the girl I've been trying to forget for fifteen years.

And it's the name looking up at me from the résumé in my hand.

Because Hannah Utley works for the company I just purchased.

And that makes her mine. Whether she likes it or not.

Dear Rosie,

Waller's Story.

Alliance Series

Dark Mafia Romance

NERO

Payton

Running away from home at seventeen wasn't easy. Let's face it, though, nothing before, or in the ten years since, has ever been easy for me.

And I'm doing okay. Sorta. I just need to keep scraping by, living under the radar. Staying out of people's way, off people's minds.

So when a man walks through my open patio door, stepping boldly into my home and my life, I should be scared. Frightened. Terrified.

But I must be more broken than I realized because I'm none of those things.

I'm intrigued.

And I'm wondering if the way to take control of my life is by giving in to him.

Nero

The first time I took a man's life, I knew there'd be no going back. No normal existence in the cards for me.

So instead of walking away, I climbed a mountain of bodies and created my own destiny. By forming The Alliance.

And I was fine with that. Content enough to carry on.

Until I stepped through those open doors and into her life.

I should've walked away. Should've gone right back out the door I came through. But I didn't.

And now her life is in danger.

But that's the thing about being a bad man. I'll happily paint the streets red to protect what's mine.

And Payton is mine. Whether she knows it or not.

KING

Okay, so, my bad for assuming the guy I was going on a date with *wasn't* married. And my bad for taking him to a friend's house for dinner, only to find out my friend is also friends with *his* wife. Because, in fact, he *is* married. And she happens to be at my friend's house because her husband was *busy working*.

Confused? So am I.

Unsurprisingly, my date's wife is super angry about finding out that her husband is a cheating asshole.

Girl, I get it.

Then, to make matters more convoluted, there is the man sitting next to my date's wife. A man named King, who is apparently her brother and who lives up to his name.

And since my *date* is a two-timing prick, I'm not going to feel bad about drooling over King,

especially since I'll never see him again.

Or at least I don't plan to.

I plan to take an Uber to the cheater's apartment to get my car keys.

I plan for it to be quick.

And if I had to list a thousand possible outcomes... witnessing my date's murder, being kidnapped by his killer, and then being forced to marry the super attractive but clearly

deranged crime lord would not have been on my Bingo card.

But alas, here I am.

DOM

VAL

When I was nine, I went to my first funeral. Along with accepting my father's death, I had to accept new and awful truths I wasn't prepared for.

When I was nineteen, I went to my mother's funeral. We weren't close, but with her gone, I became more alone than ever before.

Sure, I have a half brother who runs The Alliance. And yeah, he's given me his protection—in the form of a bodyguard and chauffeur. But I don't have anyone that really knows me. No one to really love me.

Until I meet him. The man in the airport.

And when one chance meeting turns into something hotter, something more serious, I let myself believe that maybe he's the one. Maybe this man is the one who will finally save me from my loneliness. The one to give me the family I've always craved.

DOM

The Mafia is in my blood. It's what I do.

So when that blood is spilled and one funeral turns into three, drastic measures need to be taken.

And when this battle turns into a war, I'm going to need more men. More power.

I'm going to need The Alliance.

And I'll become a member. By any means necessary.

HANS

Vengeance is rarely clean.

Sin Series

Romantic Suspense

Mr. Sin

I should have run the other way. Paid my tab and gone back to my room. But he was there. And he was... everything. I figured, what's the harm in letting passion rule my decisions for one night? So what if he looks like the Devil in a suit? I'd be leaving in the morning. Flying home, back to my pleasant but predictable life. I'd never see him again.

Except I do. In the last place I expected. And now everything I've worked so hard for is in jeopardy.

We can't stop what we've started, but this is bigger than the two of us.

And when his past comes back to haunt him, love might not be enough to save me.

Sin Too

Beth

It started with tragedy.

And secrets.

Hidden truths that refused to stay buried have come out to chase me. Now I'm on the run, living under a blanket of constant fear, pretending to be someone I'm not. And if I'm not really me, how am I supposed to know what's real?

Angelo

Watch the girl.

It was supposed to be a simple assignment. But like everything else in this family, there's nothing simple about it. Not my task. Not her fake name. And not my feelings for her.

But Beth is mine now.

So when the monsters from her past come out to play, they'll have to get through me first.

Miss Sin

I'm so sick of watching the world spin by. Of letting people think I'm plain and boring, too afraid to just be myself.

Then I see *him*.

John.

He's strength and fury and unapologetic.

He's everything I want. And everything I wish I was.

He won't want me, but that doesn't matter. The sight of him is all the inspiration I need to finally shatter this glass house I've built around myself.

Only he does want me. And when our worlds collide, details we can't see become tangled, twisting together, ensnaring us in an invisible trap.

When it all goes wrong, I don't know if I'll be able to break free of the chains binding us or if I'll suffocate in the process.

Sleet Series

Hockey Romantic Comedy

Sleet Kitten

There are a few things that life doesn't prepare you for. Like what to do when a super-hot guy catches you sneaking around in his basement. Or what to do when a mysterious package shows up with tickets to a hockey game, because apparently, he's a professional athlete. Or how to handle it when you get to the game and realize he's freaking famous since half of the 20,000 people in the stands are wearing his jersey.

I thought I was a well-adjusted adult, reasonably prepared for life. But one date with Jackson Wilder, a viral video, and a "I didn't know she was your mom" incident, and I'm suddenly questioning everything I thought I knew.

But he's fun. And great. And I think I might be falling for him. But I don't know if he's falling for me too, or if he's as much of a player off the ice as on.

Sleet Sugar

My friends have convinced me. No more hockey players.

With a dad who is the head coach for the Minnesota Sleet, it seemed like an easy decision.

My friends have also convinced me that the best way to boost my fragile self-esteem is through a one-night stand.

A dating app. A hotel bar. A sexy-as-hell man, who's sweet and funny, and did I mention, sexy as hell... I fortified my courage and invited myself up to his room.

Assumptions. There's a rule about them.

I assumed he was passing through town. I assumed he was a businessman or maybe an investor or accountant or literally anything other than a professional hockey player. I assumed I'd never see him again.

I assumed wrong.

Sleet Banshee

Mother-freaking hockey players. My friends found their happily ever afters with a couple of sweet, doting, over-the-top, in-love athletes. They got nicknames like *Kitten* and *Sugar*. But me? I got stuck with a dickhead who riles me up on purpose and calls me *Banshee*. Yeah, he might have a voice made specifically for wet dreams. And he might have a body and face carved by the gods. And he might have a level of Alpha-hole that gets me all hot and bothered.

But when he presses my buttons, he presses ALL of my buttons. And I'm not the type of girl who takes things sitting down. And I only got caught on my knees that one time. In the museum.

But when one of my decisions gets one of my friends hurt... I can't stop blaming myself. And him.

Except he can't take a hint. And I can't keep my panties on.

Sleet Princess

My trip to Mexico for my cousin's wedding was only supposed to be a few days of obligation and oceanside.

I wasn't expecting Luke.

Wasn't expecting the hot hockey player, with the smirks and the tattoos, who kept *bumping into me.*

And I certainly wasn't expecting to spend a night on the beach, under the stars, underneath *him.*

It was magical, but I thought it would end there.

Instead, we exchanged numbers and stayed in touch.

So when Luke invited me to watch him play in Vegas, I went.

And it was great.

Until we woke up the next morning and found the wedding certificate in my pocket.

Turns out that dance party we snuck into was actually a group wedding ceremony.

And now we're married.

Which is bad.

Because I think our wedding was actually our first date. And if my dad finds out, he'll cut me out of the family business.

So when footage leaks of Luke and me hot and heavy in an elevator, I have to make up a new plan to save my reputation and career.

Now, all I need is for Luke Anders to act like he's madly in love with me.

Should be easy.

Right?

Darling Series

Contemporary Small Town Romance

Smoky Darling

Elouise

I fell in love with Beckett when I was seven.

He broke my heart when I was fifteen.

When I was eighteen, I promised myself I'd forget about him.

And I did. For a dozen years.

But now he's back home. Here. In Darling Lake. And I don't know if I should give in to the temptation swirling between us or run the other way.

Beckett

She had a crush on me when she was a kid. But she was my brother's best friend's little sister. I didn't see her like that. And even if I had, she was too young. Our age difference was too great.

But now I'm back home. And she's here. And she's all the way grown up.

It wouldn't have worked back then. But I'll be damned if I won't get a taste of her now.

Latte Darling

I have a nice life—living in my hometown, owning the coffee shop I've worked at since I was sixteen.

It's comfortable.

On paper.

But I'm tired of doing everything by myself. Tired of being in charge of every decision in my life.

I want someone to lean on. Someone to spend time with. Sit with. Hug.

And I really don't want to go to my best friend's wedding alone.

So, I signed up for a dating app and agreed to meet with the first guy who messaged me.

And now here I am, at the bar.

Only it's not my date that just sat down in the chair across from me. It's his dad.

And holy hell, he's the definition of silver fox. If a silver fox can be thick as a house, have piercing blue eyes and tattoos from his neck down to his fingertips.

He's giving me *big bad wolf* vibes. Only instead of running, I'm blushing. And he looks like he might just want to eat me whole.

Tilly World Holiday Novellas

Second Bite

When a holiday baking competition goes incredibly wrong. Or right...

Michael

I'm starting to think I've been doing this for too long. The screaming fans. The constant media attention. The fat paychecks. None of it brings me the happiness I yearn for.

Yet here I am. Another year. Another holiday special. Another Christmas spent alone in a hotel room.

But then the lights go up. And I see *her*.

Alice

It's an honor to be a contestant, I know that. But right now, it feels a little like punishment. Because any second, Chef Michael Kesso, the man I've been in love with for years, the man who doesn't even know I exist, is going to walk onto the set, and it will be a miracle if I don't pass out at the sight of him.

But the time for doubts is over. Because *Second Bite* is about to start "in three... two... one..."

Printed in Great Britain
by Amazon

46604507R20076